THE LOVIN' KIND

A Morgan Family Romance

THE LOVIN' KIND

A Morgan Family Romance

•

Nancy J. Parra

Text copyright ©2006 by Nancy J. Parra
All rights reserved.
Printed in the United States of America.

Published by Montlake Romance
P.O. Box 400818
Las Vegas, NV 89140

ISBN-13: 9781612186269
ISBN-10: 1612186262

This title was previously published by Avalon Books; this version has been reproduced from Avalon Book archive files.

Chapter One

It was the most humiliating day of Beth Morgan's life.

She sat in her father's den, dressed in the beautiful wedding gown that the Boltonville Ladies Brigade had made for her sister. Only it was no longer beautiful. Covered in dust and shame, she noted that half the seed pearls that had been meticulously sewn on were missing, along with a couple of the buttons in the back. The skirt was torn at the bottom and she swore there was horse dung on the edge.

She glanced from the dress to the evil, awful man who had caused this disaster. Well, at the very least, he was the source of the horse dung.

Quaid Blair had hunted her down like a recalcitrant child, tossed her over his saddle, and brought her back home. In fact he had gone so far as to throw her over

1

his shoulder, carry her into the house, and dump her in the chair in which she currently sat. She tried to get up, merely on principle, but one threatening look from his blue eyes had warned her that it didn't matter that her father stood only a few feet away. If she got up, he'd make sure she didn't stay up.

Curse the day Quaid Blair had come into her life. The man was inhuman. She sent him a narrow-eyed glare. He ignored her. He was good at ignoring her.

For the life of her, she couldn't understand it. She was stunningly beautiful. She had known that for a fact since as far back as she could remember. All men loved her. They doted on her, waited on her hand and foot. Why, Quaid Blair had been the first man in her nearly twenty years to have been immune to her charms. It was disconcerting more than anything and not something she wanted to dwell on right now. She had bigger problems brewing.

Her father turned to her, blew out a long breath and sat down on the edge of his wide oak desk. "Tell me exactly what you were thinking," he ordered in his sternest voice, "because I haven't got a clue."

Beth felt a fresh wave of shame. Her father rarely used his stern voice and for the first time in a long time, it appeared he wouldn't be charmed out of it. Crying would have to be the next resort. She felt the sting of fat tears at the back of her eyes and let them erupt.

"Now, don't do that," he father said and fumbled for his handkerchief.

"I'm sorry," she said and she sincerely was. Sorry, humiliated, and madder than a wet hen. He handed her the square of linen. She dabbed at her eyes. "Does *he* have to be in here? This has been a very personal and trying day."

"Quaid went to all the trouble of finding you and bringing you home. The very least we owe him is an explanation of your behavior."

"I would have been so much better off if he had never found me," she said. Her tone ended in a bit of a wail. She was desperate to be done with him and with this day. Her desperation was evident in her voice. The cursed man merely crossed his arms over his chest and raised one dark dastardly eyebrow at her.

Darn it he intimidated her. She shot him a look that should have melted him to the floor and then settled on the truth. Her father was an understanding man. Surely he would understand why she had run. "Oh, Papa, it started out as such a perfect day. The sun was shining, the breeze was soft and sweet with flowers. I looked more beautiful than any bride." She paused.

"Yes, dear, you were certainly the most lovely creature," her father said and patted her on the knee. The horrid man snorted. Beth ignored him, satisfied that at least, if anything, she was lovely.

"I stepped out into the aisle and well, the church was like a storybook. Everyone was dressed in their Sunday best and smiling at me. It made me smile." She dabbed at her eyes.

"Yes, go on."

"Then I saw Hank Cartwright sitting in the aisle looking so forlorn, and Bob Metz beside him. Why, they looked like they were going to a funeral. I glanced around and saw that the Hamilton twins had been crying and Stuart Bixley was still sniffling."

"Go on . . ."

She could tell her father's patience was not what it once was. Probably due to her sisters' excessive chatter, but that was neither here nor there. She sped up her story. "Why, every man in the church looked so unhappy, except for Eric. He smiled and grinned at me as if he were the king of the world."

"Well, let's hope he felt that way. You were about to marry him."

"I know," she said and looked at her father. "I mean, when he asked me I thought I had found the love of my life."

"Why then did you run away?"

"Well, with Angus standing next to him and that sweet Tyler boy beside them, I realized that I didn't know for sure."

"What didn't you know for sure?"

"I didn't know for sure if I had picked the right man. I mean, they are all in love with me, so it was up to me to make the best choice. Papa, I don't think Eric is the best choice—at least, I'm not sure. Oh, this is simply awful." She covered her face with the kerchief and allowed her tears to fall. Sobs so real they frightened her burst forth from her chest. "I'm so confused. It just seemed like one big terrible mistake."

"So, you turned tail and ran."

"I didn't know what else to do," she said and her breath hitched. She looked up and pleaded for her father to understand. "I mean, I saw Maddie and she looked so happy sitting next to Trevor. Then Amelia, wearing her lying-in clothes and I thought that could soon be me. I mean, in just a few short months I could be carrying Eric's child and I'd be as big as a good-sized heifer. None of the other boys would even recognize me." The idea of losing her seventeen-and-a-half-inch waist was enough to stun her silly. She caught a painful sob so that it came out like more of a hiccup. The handkerchief went under her nose. "I was out the door and down the street before I even realized it."

"So, this is simply a case of cold feet," her father concluded.

"A serious case," the unwelcome man said. "She stole a horse that was tied up outside the grocer and was headed for the hills."

"I'm so ashamed," she wailed and kept her eyes on her father. "Can't you see how humiliated I feel? The ladies were so kind to put everything together. The ceremony, the bridal showers, it was all so much fun."

"Right up until the time you had to go through with your pledge."

She turned and glared at Quaid. "I was blinded by everyone's enthusiasm."

"And the hundred dollar diamond that boy slipped on your finger."

She glanced down at her engagement ring. It was the biggest, most beautiful ring she had ever seen. Her sisters didn't own anything so lovely. It struck her suddenly that she would have to give it up.

Fresh tears rushed into her eyes and she bit her handkerchief to keep from wailing. The price for all her fun, for the household gifts, the new clothes, the diamond, was simply too high. She would have to become Mrs. Eric Slausser—the wife of an accountant. Somehow she had thought to become so much more.

She turned her tear-filled eyes on her father. "I wasn't ready."

"I see that." Her father paced in front of her. "The boy's family was aghast at your behavior. I doubt I will ever do business with them again."

"Oh, Papa, have I ruined a sale?"

"It's not so important," he said and waved the thought aside. Then he hunkered down in front of her and took her hands. "What is important is that you realized your mistake before you actually made it."

There was a knock at the door and Mrs. Poole, the Morgan's housekeeper, opened the door to the den. "I'm sorry to interrupt, but there are people in the parlor waiting to speak with you, sir."

"I'm sure there are," her father answered. He went to rise but Beth clung to him.

"I can't see anyone, Papa. Not now, not like this."

"You have to face them," her father said. "You have to explain yourself."

"I can't," she whispered. The very thought of facing Eric and his parents terrified her more than the man in the corner.

Her father looked into her eyes and blew out a breath. "All right. I'll handle them tonight, but first thing tomorrow, you'll have to make your amends."

"I can't see them, Papa. Ever." She wrung her hands together. "That's why I ran. I can never show my face in Boltonville again."

"Now you're being overdramatic." Her father patted her hands. "I'm sure come tomorrow, you'll feel better."

"I'm never going to feel better," she swore. "Look at me, I ran away on my wedding day. I can never show my face in town again."

"Well, now, you can't spend the rest of your life locked up in my house."

"I won't," she said. "I can't."

Her father frowned and straightened. "I suppose you could go live with your aunts for a while."

Beth blanched at the idea. Her two spinster aunts lived in a small town in Michigan. They were an odd pair that kept far too many cats. Their house smelled oddly as well. The thought of ending up in Regency dress with blue hair was almost as unnerving as the vision she had of being pregnant with Eric Slausser's child.

"No!"

Her father's gaze landed on her. "There is no other choice."

"Yes, there is," she said and stood with the force of her opinion. "I want to go to Wyoming to live with Robert."

"What?"

"Wyoming is the perfect solution. Robert said it is the most beautiful place he's ever seen. Just last month he was asking you to come see it. In fact he wants us all to live there. We could sell the house and move right away."

"I can't go to Wyoming right now. I have several business transactions here and in Chicago."

"Then I can take a train," she said and grabbed her father's sleeve. "There's a train that goes out to Cheyenne."

"A young woman cannot travel that far alone."

"Yes, I can."

"No, you can't."

"I see, so I am capable of getting married and having children," she started, then paused at the sound of a snort from Mr. Blair and glared at him. Quaid responded with a raised eyebrow. She ignored it and pressed on, "But I'm incapable of traveling by myself."

"Precisely."

"How incredibly insane."

"The truth is the truth, young lady."

She rolled her eyes. She could feel the burden of

staying in Boltonville pressing down upon her. "Then send Henry with me."

"Henry is at university. I won't take him out of his semester just because you can't face the Slaussers."

"Please Papa, I can't stay here." She was desperate, nearly desperate enough to go live with her aunts, though the thought chilled her.

Her father paced the room. He stopped and glanced at Mrs. Poole. "Tell them I'll be right out."

"Yes, sir," she said and quietly closed the door behind her.

Robert Morgan turned and eyed his daughter. "You have a problem."

"It's an awful problem," she said with a quick nod, "but so much better than marrying the wrong man. Please Papa, let me go to Wyoming, just for the next year or so until Eric finds another love."

"You think the Slaussers will forget that you ran out on their boy by Christmas?"

Beth winced. "I can write Carrie a letter. She has been in love with Eric for as long as we have known him."

"Your best friend is in love with your fiancé?"

"Yes."

"And you were going to marry him anyway?"

"Of course, he wanted me not Carrie."

"But you clearly aren't in love with him."

"No. I thought I was, but it became suddenly clear to

me that I was making a big mistake. Carolyn can have him. She will love him until the day he dies. Why, just three months ago she was dreaming of babies with Eric's green eyes."

"Babies you don't want to have."

She simply looked at her father. It wouldn't do to repeat herself. Robert Morgan blew out a breath. "You are the most irresponsible twit I have ever known."

She ducked the shame that came from his words. "Please Papa, send me to Wyoming. I can be packed and ready tonight. I promise I will post a nice long apology to the Slaussers and a heart-filled letter to Eric."

"In which you will enclose your ring."

She glanced down at the beautiful diamond. "Surely he would want me to keep it."

"You will put it in the post with a very long letter of apology."

"And you will go with me to Wyoming?"

"I told you, I cannot go." Her father paused. "But it just so happens that Quaid here is leaving in a few days to take some mares out to Wyoming."

"Quaid?" She refused to look at the man. Surely her father had lost his mind. "Surely there must be someone else who can escort me." She grabbed her father's arm and leaned in close. "The man despises me."

"Good," her father said with the cold sound of finality. "Then I won't have to worry about another one of your ridiculous romances."

She flinched. Romance and Quaid were the last two

things she would ever put together. The thought was as
foreign to her as, well, as leaping off a cliff just for fun.

"I can't wait a couple of days," she wailed. "If I don't
leave soon I'll never leave."

Her father shook his head and frowned. "Would you
be ready to leave at dawn?" he asked Quaid.

Beth closed her eyes and prayed for the word no.

"I'm ready to go whenever."

"What about right now," she said turning to her
father. "I want to leave right now, tonight."

"Don't be ridiculous."

"I could be persuaded to leave tonight," Quaid said
quietly.

Beth shot him a look of disbelief. "Fine. I can be
ready in one hour."

"I'll be ready in fifteen minutes."

"My steamer trunk is already packed."

"You'll ship the trunk and bring your carpetbag.
You'll also need riding clothes. I presume you do ride."

"Of course I ride. You saw me riding just this afternoon."

"What I saw was a willful, spoiled child stealing an
innocent man's horse and running away."

"I was not stealing."

"Really?"

"Really." She turned her back on the hateful man. "I
can be ready in a half hour. Please Papa, I need time to
think, and I can't think here, not while the entire town
is watching me."

Her father looked over her shoulder at the man behind her. "It's nearing dark."

"The animals are well rested."

"Please Papa, please." Beth allowed big tears to fill her eyes. "I promise not to ask anything else of you."

Her father gave a short bark of a laugh. "Now I don't believe that." He patted her on the shoulder. "Fine. If you can be ready in thirty minutes, you can go. Now scoot. Go find Mrs. Poole and ask her to help you."

For the first time that day, she relaxed a little. She kissed her father on the cheek, picked up her tattered skirt and moved to the door.

"I'm leaving in exactly thirty minutes," Quaid said soft and sure. "It's nothing to me to leave you here if you're not ready."

That got her back up. If there was one thing a Morgan couldn't abide was a challenge. "Oh, I'll be ready."

He leaned against the wall and crossed his arms over his chest. "We'll see about that."

She gasped at his audacity. He merely watched her. "Time's awastin'."

"Well!" She hurried through the door. She caught Mrs. Poole in the hallway. "Mrs. Poole, please, I need your help."

"Are you going to speak to your young man? He's in the parlor with his parents. He looks so sad."

"I'm sure Eric will be just fine," Beth said and took the housekeeper's pudgy arm. "We'll take the back way up to my room. I have to rearrange my packing. I can't take my steamer trunk. Papa says you'll have to ship it. My carpetbag was packed for my honeymoon. None of that will do for a trip to Wyoming. I'm going to have to completely redo everything," she babbled as she dragged the old woman up the stairs. "Oh my, and I have some serious letter writing to do."

"Hmmm, you certainly do."

"Don't worry, Mr. Morgan, she'll be back by breakfast," Quaid said. He was as sure of this fact as he was that his grandmother had been shanty Irish. A woman as spoiled as Beth Morgan wouldn't take kindly to being driven hundreds of miles across the prairie. "Dinner at the latest."

"What do you intend?"

"I intend to take those horses to Wyoming by trail. I wouldn't risk those beauties on a cattle car. We'll be riding to Wyoming by the seat of our pants. Once we get out of Wisconsin, there's nothing much between here and there but tall prairie grass and open sky."

Robert Morgan lifted one corner of his mouth in a serious chuckle. "You plan on introducing her to the realities of the West."

"Yes, sir, I do."

"You'll treat her right." The old man narrowed his eyes.

"Yes, sir, just like my own kid sister," Quaid replied. Beth may be the most beautiful creature he'd ever seen, but that wasn't enough to turn his head. Hothouse flowers weren't his thing. Now, give him a sturdy prairie rose, something with grit and determination—that was more his style. He mentally shook his head. Beth Morgan was as fragile as an orchid. She'd be lucky to make it farther than an hour out of town.

"You're going to have to slip out of town," Robert said with a sigh. He reached down and pulled a cigar out of his box, sniffed it, bit off the end and lit it. He offered the box to Quaid who took two and slipped them in his pocket.

Robert leaned against his desk, blew out a ring of smoke and shook his head. "I wouldn't be surprised if there were half a dozen men already in the parlor waiting to find out what happened." He puffed on the cigar. "Maybe it's best to get her out of town." He glanced at Quaid. "I know my daughters, son. Beth may surprise you and make it to Wyoming."

Quaid shrugged. "Then I'll drop her off with Robert."

"Fine." He eyed Quaid. "She's a handful and I know you weren't expecting it."

"Don't you have any worries, sir," Quaid said softly. "I'm the best trail man around and I have no designs on the gal."

"I trust you like I trust my own sons or I would have never sold you those horses," Robert Morgan said. "But just so we're clear, anything happens to my baby and I won't be the only one coming after you, and it won't be anything as quick and easy as a bullet through your heart."

"I wouldn't expect anything else out of you or your men."

The old man snuffed his cigar out in the big glass ashtray on top of his desk. "Good, good." He straightened and tugged on his waistcoat. "Time to go and face the out-laws," he muttered and patted Quaid on the back. "You've never disappointed me, son, I don't expect you'll start now."

Quaid watched as the old man left the room. He took a deep breath, blew it out slowly and tugged his old battered trail hat down over his head. He glanced at the mantle clock. He had another twenty minutes before they left. Time enough to gather up the supplies the horses needed and set off on the trail. With any luck they'd make ten miles before nightfall. After a night of bunking out on the cold hard ground, he figured they'd be heading right back.

It would be an interesting little journey, taking no more than a day out of his schedule. Someone had to give that spoiled little gal a taste of reality. Better him than some scallywag con man. The way Quaid saw it, Elizabeth Morgan would need a strong hand to corral her and he was the man for the job.

Chapter Two

Twenty eight minutes later, Beth led her favorite mare out of the barn. The animal carried what Beth considered a journey's worth of packing. Her small carpetbag was attached to the side of her saddle. She had packed her camping gear just in case they didn't make it to a town and had to camp out one night. She glanced at the small watch pinned to her breast and nodded with pride.

She was ready in less than thirty minutes. Why, she'd show Quaid a thing or two. She stepped out into the early spring evening. Quaid sat atop his big stallion. His battered cowman's hat topped his head. He leaned down on the pummel of his saddle and eyed the horizon.

For a moment her heart went still in her breast. His

was the silhouette of an elemental man—long, lean, and powerful as a panther. She knew that he would be the one man who would stand between her and harm on this journey. For a moment she wondered if she was wrong to despise him.

Then he turned and caught sight of her. "If you're having second thoughts, you might just as well turn around and unpack that mare."

That got her moving. She mounted her animal. "Let's go."

She thought she caught a hint of a grin on him before he turned and hitched his reins. It was enough to make her grumpy. The man simply loved to bother her. Darn it, it was going to be a very long trip to Wyoming.

She blew out a breath and refused to glance back. She knew she would see her father's house disappearing behind her. In so many ways she was torn. She loved that house, loved Boltonville and the people. That's how she had gotten into this mess—she simply loved everyone, especially the attention young men showed her. How could she ever choose just one?

She closed her mind to the horrors of the day. Instead she concentrated on the horror in front of her. Quaid's horse pushed ahead. He had four mares hitched to his horse. All four animals carried packs. She wondered what was in their packs. Then she glanced at the hateful man who ignored her as he headed through the woods behind her father's house and figured she wouldn't ask him. No, she would simply do some snooping when they stopped for the night. The silence of their ride didn't bother her. She didn't want to talk to Quaid anyway. She didn't want to hear his opinion, to know that he disapproved of her right down to the boots she wore.

No one ever disapproved of her. It was disconcerting. Quaid Blair had taken one look at her and had frowned. It was a puzzle she couldn't piece together. She had done nothing to him. There was no particular reason for it except that he simply didn't like her. The man must be crazy.

She blew out a sigh. The entire day had been crazy. She had been so sure she was doing the right thing. There had been so much love and pride in her heart when Eric had courted her. It had been so much fun to hold his hand and let him steal kisses from her in the dark. He was tall and handsome and promised her he'd be wealthy. From the looks of his parents' status, he was already well on his way.

Everyone had congratulated her on the engagement. They went on and on about how lucky she was, how beautiful the diamond was. She glanced down at her gloved hand. She had put the ring back in its box and had left it for Mrs. Poole to send with the letter to Eric she had quickly composed before leaving. She swallowed hard. In that aspect Quaid had been horribly right. It had been more difficult to give up the ring than to give up Eric.

She didn't want to dwell on that thought too much. After all, the world simply must be coming to an end if Quaid was right. She took another deep breath and looked around. The air was heavy with spring. Humidity made the plants thrive and her hair curl. It smelled of fresh leaves and loamy pine from the forest floor.

May apples and ferns brushed the horses as they rode by. Blue jays squawked and shrieked at them. Robins peeped to let them know they were too close to a nest. Mosquitoes buzzed in the air and she was thankful for the denim jacket she wore over her linen blouse. It may have been warm, but it kept the insects at bay.

The air around them grew dark with shadows as the sun set. Deer grazed along the edge of the woods and bounded away from them when they came too close. She had a sudden terrifying thought. "Do you think we'll run into any bears?"

Quaid turned and looked at her with dark expressionless eyes. She couldn't read his mood. That alone was strange. She was usually very good at reading other people.

"I have a rifle if we run into anything dangerous."

"I have a pistol too," she said. "That wasn't what I asked. I asked if you thought we'd run into any bears."

"You have a pistol?"

"Yes."

"What kind?"

"A Colt six-shooter."

"Why?"

"Why? What an odd question."

"Just answer it."

Impatient with him, Beth huffed. "I have a pistol to protect myself."

"Do you know how to use it?"

"Of course I know how to use it," she mocked. "I wouldn't wear it if I didn't know how to use it."

"Maybe you should ride ahead of me."

"Why?"

"So you don't accidentally shoot me in the back."

"Don't worry," she said. "I won't shoot you unless I mean too."

He let that comment go. She was glad. The man really got on her nerves. Of course she knew how to shoot—she was a Morgan after all. Her Papa wouldn't have any one of his girls so helpless that they couldn't protect themselves, which is why she had been surprised her father had required her to have an escort to go to Wyoming.

She sighed. Maybe she didn't have to have an escort. It was clear that Quaid was as unhappy as she was with the situation. "You know, you don't have to escort me if you don't want."

"I do and I will."

"Seriously, you can take me to the next train station. I am certain there is a perfectly comfortable train from here to Cheyenne."

"I won't put these horses in a cattle car. It's too dangerous," he replied. "We'll ride the trail."

"You can still ride the trail. You can even watch me get on the train if you like. I'll be fine. I have my gun and enough money to pay for the ticket plus a week's worth of meals."

"Look, I've been on those trains. Young women don't ride them alone and there's good reason."

She blew out a breath. "If you're afraid Papa won't pay you if you don't escort me, be sure that I can match whatever amount he promised you."

He turned and eyed her. "I don't do business with women."

"Oh, well . . ." She pondered that improbability for a moment. "Why not?"

"It's a family thing."

"I see." She rode a ways and watched the night sky turn from blue to black. Her horse stuck with the line of mares behind Quaid as they found the road and traveled west. "How about if my brother, Robert, pays you."

"Well, now that'd be between me and Robert, and since he's not here, I doubt that will be happening."

"Come on, I can telegraph him. He'll be fine with it."

Quaid didn't answer. The sound of night insects grew loud. Somewhere a coyote howled. The lonely sound sent a shiver down her spine. She refused to complain, even if it meant riding all night long. This had been her choice and she would live with the consequences at least until she could figure out how to change them.

Quaid settled into the long ride like a man settles into his favorite chair. For him, the open road was his life. Ever since the war he had come to rely on the freedom of the wilderness. He'd come from money and soon realized that with money came responsibility. So, he had decided to live a carefree, nomadic life.

But it hadn't worked out that way. It all began when he won a silver mine in a poker game. Within a week of owning it, the mine had hit pay dirt. He sold it right after and invested the money in what he'd hoped were a couple of surefire losers. Within a month he had tripled his wealth.

Someone had once told him ranching was a terrible gamble. In an effort to lose his fortune he bought a ranch in Colorado, and another in Wyoming. But before he knew it he had become the richest man in five states.

In those days it seemed everything he touched turned to gold. Quaid gave up trying to lose his wealth. He found himself swamped with so-called friends and women who eyed him more for the money in his wallet than the worth of his heart.

That got old fast and, once again, Quaid took to the trail. There was something simple and sacred about riding alone. Hiring on to some poor man's place and working a full day's hard labor just for the thrill of it. Women like Beth would never understand the need to wander. They were rooted to their societies, planted in their homes and churches. Women like Beth Morgan had one thing on their minds and that was their creature comforts and their fine clothes.

Quaid wasn't interested in those kinds of women. He thought about his mother and grandmother. They were good women with big hearts who worked alongside their men, even after they came into money.

Quaid glanced at the spoiled gal beside him. Beth had probably never worked a day in her life. He'd watched how everyone coddled her and took care of her. He'd seen the gleam in her eye whenever she looked at her engagement ring.

Nope. Beth Morgan might be beautiful but she was not Quaid's idea of marrying material. The way he figured it, Slausser would eventually be glad she ran out on him.

Quaid scratched his chin. Women like Beth were rarely worth the price a man paid when he married them.

It was something he had to remind himself every time he caught himself staring at the brilliant blue of her eyes or the astonishingly beautiful curve of her face.

Just on principle, Quaid pushed them farther than he should have, farther than he would have had he been by himself. From the look of the sky, it had to be well past midnight. He glanced back to see that Beth could barely keep her head up. Still she hadn't complained . . . yet.

He chuckled. She was a stubborn thing. He stood up

in his stirrups and stretched. His own backside had begun to protest and he knew that he couldn't push the horses like this the entire way. It was time to camp for the night.

He dismounted, pulled his saddle off his animal and rubbed him down. Placing a handful of oats in a feeder he slipped it over the stallion's head. Then he unhitched the mares, pulled off their packs, and piled everything in a neat circle. He gave each of the mares a carrot then hobbled them.

After all that, he turned to Beth. Her animal was well trained and docile. She simply stood and waited her turn. Beth herself had been sleeping in her saddle unaware that they had been stopped for so long.

Quaid took a deep breath and blew it out slowly. For a brief moment he thought about making a bed for her and putting her in it himself, but that would defeat his purpose. Instead he smacked her on the leg.

"What!" She woke up startled.

"We're stopping for the night. You need to take care of your animal."

She blinked at him. "What?"

"Get down and take care of your horse. We're off again at sunrise and your mare deserves some rest."

"Oh."

He had to turn his back on her. She looked so sweet, all drowsy and flustered. It was all he could do not to take care of her. That was the whole problem. He bet every single man and woman who ever met Beth Morgan took one look at her and wanted to take care of her. It's why she was so darned spoiled. If he started in on caring now, it would never stop and it wouldn't do the gal any good.

Deliberately, he moved away, laying out his bedroll. He put his saddle at the head and laid down. There was a chill to the damp night air, but he wouldn't make a fire. The more uncomfortable he made her, the sooner she would stop this whole charade.

Instead he ignored her as she huffed. He covered his eyes with his hat and pretended to sleep, using his imagination to match the sounds she made to her movements. He heard her struggling to dismount. He waited for her to realize she had to get that forty-pound saddle off her mare by herself.

Quaid knew he could be cold-hearted when it suited him and right now it suited him. So, his head resting on his saddle, he listened to her struggle. She whispered a few curses that had him raising an eyebrow under the cover of his hat. There was a loud thud as she managed to get the saddle off her horse. From the sound of it, she must have ended up on her backside at the effort.

He grinned as she muttered under her breath and struggled to get up. It was tempting to take off his hat and watch her, but that would only rub salt on her wound. It was better she think he ignored her.

He listened while she huffed out a breath. Then she picked herself up and finished her chores. In the end he heard her horse munching on a carrot and Beth talking low and sweet to the animal.

For a brief moment, he imagined what it would be like if she were to talk low and sweet to him. It was a trap of course, one he would never fall into, but that didn't keep him from imagining what it would be like. While he was daydreaming, she snuck up on him and kicked his leg. Pain shot up his shin. He sat up suddenly, pulled his hat off his face, and frowned at her. "What?"

"Aren't you going to make a fire?"

"Why?"

"To keep us warm," she said and crossed her arms over her breast like a demanding queen.

"Nope."

"No?"

"Nope."

"Why not?" She sounded exhausted and more than a bit exasperated. He kind of liked that. It meant something to know he could get under the princess's skin.

"Waste of time, dawn will be here in less than four hours."

"Oh." She glanced around as if lost. "Well."

"Get some sleep," he ordered. "We're leaving at dawn." He glanced at her. "You'd better be ready."

"Oh, I'll be ready."

"Good." He lay back down, put his hat back over his face, and pretended to sleep. He continued to listen as she stood there debating what to do next. Finally, she dragged her saddle across from him, laid out her blankets and curled up in them.

He wondered what she was thinking, but decided it didn't really matter. Once she understood that she would have to take care of herself, she'd be running back to her father soon enough. He yawned. Then he could head out for real.

In the meantime, it would be fun to see just how far he could push her before she cracked. Yep, he thought. Crack of dawn he'd be leaving. By tomorrow night, she'll be begging him to turn around and take her back home. He made a bet with himself that she wouldn't even make it out of Wisconsin.

The ground was hard and dew settled onto her, making her clothes damp and heavy. She rolled over and a sharp-edged rock jammed into her hip. Darn it, she had been camping before but nothing had been as terrible as these cold dark hours at the edge of the road.

She dreamed of home, of her soft bed, and waking up next to Eric. The dream suddenly became a nightmare. Eric's beautiful hair disappeared, his front teeth too. In the dream, he grinned at her with a lecherous look and feral breath. "Good morning, darling," he said and ran his hand along her bare shoulder. "Are you ready to make a baby?"

She shrunk away from the nightmare. "No," she whispered. "No."

"But that's what we got married for, honey," Eric remarked, "to pepper the landscape with younguns."

"Oh, no," she whispered and tossed on the hard

ground, jamming her elbow. She woke up with a start and sat up straight. Her heart raced, sweat beaded on her forehead. *My goodness, what a nightmare.* It took her a moment to figure out where she was and remind herself that she had had the good sense to escape before the nightmare had become real.

"It's about time you got up." The sound of Quaid's deep voice startled her. "It's nearly dawn. You'd better see to your animal."

She blinked and tried to find him in the dark. She turned to his voice and made out a shadow against the black night. Stars still blanketed the sky. "What do you mean it's dawn, we just stopped."

"The sun's already rising," he said. "By the time you get your horse saddled it will be mid-morning. Get started now, unless of course, you're ready to go back."

"I'm not going back," she said and stood up. "I'll be ready to leave by the time the sun's up."

"See that you are."

She really didn't like that man. He had her over a barrel and they both knew it. It looked as if he was going to push her the whole way. She stretched, desperate to drive the kinks out of her back and, blowing out a deep breath, Beth picked up her blankets and clucked to her horse.

The beautiful mare came right to her. She patted her sweet ride, whispered small comforts, promising her sugar when they made it to Robert's. Then she folded her blankets and tossed them over the mare's back.

Methodically, she saddled her horse. It had been a long, long time since she'd had to do it herself. Usually she'd had one of her father's men do it for her. If she was away from home, there was always a ready hand waiting to help her. The price really hadn't been that much—a simple smile and kind word and the helpful men had gone away happy.

It seemed like such a little thing. Something Quaid Blair would not understand. The weight of the saddle had her grunting and, though she did stagger a bit, her mare waited patiently. She ended up dragging the saddle over to the animal. She glanced over to see Quaid leaning against a tree watching her. Even in the dim light of early morning, she could see that he was laughing at her.

"I'll saddle her for you if you forget this nonsense and promise to go home," he offered.

"I can do it," she said. "It's just been awhile," she muttered the last bit under her breath. Determined, she gritted her teeth and picked up the heavy saddle. Surely she couldn't be this weak. The effort to lift it to shoulder height had sweat breaking out on her forehead and it was not warm outside.

Her heart pounded and her arm muscles screamed. Then she remembered her dream and knew that she had a choice here. She could give up and go home and go bear Eric's children, or she could work through the muscle pain and get this saddle onto the back of her horse.

She attacked the task with renewed strength and managed to barely inch the saddle over the back of her mare. She pushed and shoved and worked it until it was finally in place. She rested against the animal's side. Her entire body trembled from the effort. Her heartbeat sounded like a drum in her ears.

"Don't stop now. Sun's almost up." Quaid had the audacity to whisper into her ear, sending a different kind of shiver down her spine. She turned her head to send him an evil look, but the man had walked away from her. He climbed up on his stallion with one easy motion and leaned on his pummel. "We'll wait until sunrise. If you aren't properly saddled by then the decision will be made for you."

She hated the bland look in his eye. He had no mercy. Beth looked at her handiwork. The saddle had pushed most of the blanket off the other side of the horse. "I said I would have her saddled and I'll have her saddled. Why don't you do something useful like make coffee."

He laughed then. The sound made her smile despite herself. "Honey, you can't make coffee without fire and what we have here is a cold camp. If you need something to drink, there's water in your canteen." He glanced at the sky. "You'd better get moving, especially if you need to stop in the bushes. Time's quickly running out."

Beth felt a moment of panic. She refused to go back home and there was so much to do. She scrambled to adjust the blanket under the heavy saddle, then cinched the saddle and checked to make sure it was completely secure. She glanced at the sky and watched the pink streaks turn to orange. In a moment the ball of early sun would be peaking over the horizon.

She finished her final adjustments and then made a mad dash to the bushes.

"Better make it quick. Sun says it's time to go, unless of course you want to go back to Boltonville."

She hated the happy tone of his voice. She really did. Beth came out of the bushes, hooking her belt. She hated to think what a fright she must look, but then again maybe if he saw how bad she looked, he'd have pity on her and give her some time for her toilet.

She mounted her mare, taking note that he did not come over to help her as any gentleman would. Good thing she had been riding horses practically all her life. She adjusted her seat, picked up her reins, and saw that he was already halfway down the road.

For a brief moment she was sorely tempted to go the other way. Surely she could find a town with a train station. That would show him.

"Don't even think it," his voice floated across the air. "My stallion is faster than your mare. If I have to, I'll catch you and make you ride with me."

The thought sent shivers down her back. Disgruntled, she urged her mare forward and quickly caught up with him. The sun rose bright and true, the soft pinks of dawn displacing the darker shadows.

Birds chirped their territorial songs and the road was quiet.

She took a deep breath and realized that this was a journey to find her destiny. She knew with more certainty now that she wasn't suited to life as an accountant's wife. What she needed was adventure. She smiled at her realization. The sheer romance of the idea, of the freedom to be found in the West lifted her heart.

If there was one thing Beth loved it was romance. That was what had gotten her into trouble in Boltonville. She loved the romance of courting more than its realities. She frowned briefly and hoped that she didn't find the same thing to be true about the romance of adventure.

Chapter Three

Beth's romance of adventure wore off by mid-morning. She picked up her canteen and swallowed a mouthful of stale, lukewarm water. Right now she'd give anything for a good thick cup of coffee, better yet a hot meal with bacon and eggs and those wonderful muffins Mrs. Poole made every morning. Why, she'd slather butter on them and let it melt until it disappeared. Then she'd spread strawberry jam on top. The first bite would taste like pure heaven.

She blew out a long breath and opened her eyes. There was no meal in sight. Since she'd had to skip dinner the night before, she felt a bit faint.

Beth eyed the back of the man who rode so carelessly in front of her. It didn't seem to bother him at all that they hadn't eaten. She wondered if she should say something or simply fall off her horse in a dead faint.

The idea had some appeal. Perhaps then he would feel guilty for treating her like a ranch hand instead of a lady. She waved a fly away from the front of her face and realized that her nose hurt. She wrinkled it. Yes, it did indeed hurt. She glanced up to see that the sun was nearing its peak. It was clear that her precaution of wearing a hat would not prevent her from getting sunburned.

Good lord, she was going to look like a heathen by the time she arrived at Robert's new home. She would be lucky if he recognized her at all.

"Excuse me," Beth spoke up.

"Yes?" came a lazy masculine reply.

"How much longer before we stop?"

"Why would we need to stop?"

What kind of question was that? She frowned and the effort tugged at her pinkened skin. "Well, the horses need to rest. Surely you don't plan to walk them to death before we even arrive in Wyoming."

"Honey, we aren't even out of Wisconsin yet."

"Are we on some kind of deadline?"

He looked at the sky, then turned and looked at her. The deep gaze of his clear blue eyes penetrated hers and for a moment she sizzled as if her entire body had been left out in the sun. It was a strange sensation. She couldn't decide if she liked it or hated it.

"It's a heck of a long way to Wyoming, darlin'. If

you're bored or tired already then we might just as well head back to Boltonville."

"I wasn't asking to turn back," she said, allowing a little of the exasperation she was feeling to enter her tone. She waved again at the pesky fly. "I was wondering when we were going to stop. I don't want my mare to be overcome with heat."

He looked Beth up and down and then did the same with her horse. "You and your mare will be just fine. There's a stream a few miles up ahead. We'll stop and let the animals drink, then it's back to the trail. We've a long way to go and we won't get there by dilly dallying."

"I do not dilly dally," she said, irritated with his condescending tone.

"There won't be any traipsing about, either."

She gasped. "I will have you know that I have never traipsed."

"Lollygagging, then."

"A Morgan does not dilly dally, traipse, or lollygag. We are purposeful people. Once we set on a task we see it through to the end."

"Right. That's why you're not married."

Ouch. That hurt. She closed her mouth with a snap. She'd show him. She was a Morgan and made of sterner stuff. Just because she had had the good sense to flee before she made a terrible error did not mean she was fuzzy-headed. If she had to she would sit on her horse and burn to a crisp. Then he'd see what kind of stuff she was made of.

She waved at that fly one more time and let her temper simmer. It was hot, she had had little sleep, and she hadn't eaten. Just let him try to mess with her. She paused a moment, her eye on the prize and then with a quick flick of her wrist, she caught the darn bug. Victory was quickly squashed by what to do with the creature that buzzed in the palm of her gloved hand. She didn't have the heart to kill it. If she let it go, it would continue to annoy her just like that horrid man who led the way down the road. She blew out a breath and wished that she could talk to the stupid bug and tell it to leave her alone. She then imagined its answer would be quite smart. *If you won't kill me, why should I do what you want?* The idea of being talked back to by a fly furthered her irritation.

Shoot, she couldn't let a fly outwit her. If she refused to kill it, it would do just that. She had to put up with Quaid, but she wasn't about to let a fly make her do something she didn't want to do. She reached into her skirt pocket and produced a linen handkerchief. With a quick flick of her wrist, she shook the fly off and quickly covered her face with the kerchief until only her eyes showed. Then she tied the linen behind her neck.

The covering worked quite nicely to deflect the fly and also to keep the sun off her delicate skin. Now all she had to do was figure out what to do about the hole hunger had gnawed in her stomach. She wished she had had the good sense to pack some journey cake or even some jerky. Anything to stave off the rumble in her stomach.

She sighed, then noticed that Quaid appeared to be eating something. She narrowed her eyes and kicked her mare to catch up with him. Sure enough, he had a fistful of jerky. He ignored her pointed stare and took a huge bite out of the dried meat.

The sight of that jerky was something to behold. It made her mouth water and her stomach rumble. He took another bite, oblivious to the fact that she rode beside him. The man was clearly an unmannered boar. If he were any kind of man at all he would have seen to it that she got something to eat first.

"Is something the matter?" he finally asked and glanced at her.

"Are you going to continue to eat that in front of me without sharing?"

He raised a dark eyebrow. "I suppose you've already eaten through your supplies and now want to mooch off me."

"Supplies, what supplies? I don't have any . . ."

"Are you telling me that you didn't pack any food?"

"Well, of course I didn't pack any food. You are the leader of this little expedition. I assumed you would have the forethought to pack enough for both of us." Now her temper was up. How dare he suggest that she had been foolish. He never told her she was to pack her own food.

"You assumed I was going to feed you? What made you think that?"

"Because a gentleman always looks out for a lady."

He turned a doleful gaze on her. "I don't see any ladies."

She felt her eyes widen and her jaw drop at the insult. If she had been closer, she'd have slapped him.

"You had better explain yourself right now."

"Or what? You'll turn around and go home?"

"That's what you want, isn't it? Well, you are going to be sadly disappointed. I am not going back there."

"I highly doubt you'll make it to Wyoming without any food."

"I have money. I'll purchase some when we reach the nearest town."

"We're not going through any towns."

"You are purposefully being hateful."

"Listen, there's just the two of us. If we drag through every town between here and Cheyenne, someone's going to take one look at these mares and get the idea they can take them from us. I, for one, am not stupid enough to do that."

She hated it when he sounded logical. She couldn't argue around it without sounding terribly self-centered. Her stomach growled. "Fine then, I will go into town by myself."

"No, you won't."

"What do you mean, no?"

He looked her up and down. The heat in his gaze

made her cheeks flaming hot. "Even with that silly ker-chief covering your face, some idiot is going to see a pretty young thing in expensive clothes. Then he's going to see that you are alone."

"I suppose you believe he'll try to kidnap and rav-ish me."

"Not *he*," Quid said baldly, "*them*."

The idea of more than one man grabbing her made her mouth go dry.

"You are not going into town alone."

Tears welled up in the back of her eyes. She blinked them back and straightened her spine. "Fine. Then I'll pay you for half of your supplies."

He ran his tongue around his teeth and eyed her thoughtfully. "I don't know. Half a man's supplies out in the wilderness is worth a lot. I doubt you have enough cash to cover it."

"I'll offer you twenty dollars."

He laughed and took a bit of his jerky. "I'm not starving for twenty dollars."

"Forty?"

"Nope."

"Fifty is all I have."

"A man can't survive on money."

"You are unbelievable. I promise, Robert will pay you a hundred dollars once you deliver me safely to his door. I think that is more than reasonable."

"One hundred dollars and that mare you're riding."

Beth gasped. Buttercup had been hers since she was

born. Beth had seen to her training and personally seen to every detail in her keeping. Buttercup was her only pet, her only real possession now that she had abandoned her dowry. "I'll starve thank you."

He shrugged. "No skin off my nose. Let me know if you change your mind."

"I will not change my mind, no matter how hateful you are."

"Suit yourself."

Beth allowed her mare to drop back and ride side by side with one of the mares. She was so angry she wanted to shoot something. The way things were going she would have to conserve her bullets, for it was a cinch that that man would not save her if she ran out of bullets and an Indian decided to haul her off. Really, how could Papa trust him so much?

She eyed the full packs on the backs of the mares. Surely he had food packed in there somewhere. She glanced at Quaid's back. If he wasn't going to share, then she would simply have to pinch some when he wasn't looking. She just had to find a time when he wasn't looking.

Quaid had a heck of a time not laughing out loud. Really, the look on her face when he told her she was supposed to have packed her own food . . . it was priceless. He popped the last bit of jerky in his mouth and enjoyed the rich smoky flavor of the hardened meat.

He figured she was so badly spoiled she would be

pitching a fit at any moment. Then he'd simply turn to her and tell her she had two choices: Go home or shut up and go forward. It didn't take much imagination to hear her say that she had had enough and take her home. When she did, he'd stop, make her coffee and a solid breakfast, then turn around.

He glanced up at the sky. It was a bright blue. The humidity was thick and fat flies buzzed around the horses. Yup, she'd have enough any minute now. He closed his eyes and imagined his triumph. He wouldn't gloat, though. He was man enough not to do it in front of her anyway.

He took a deep breath and blew it out slowly. He hoped she gave in soon. Quaid missed his morning coffee.

Three hours later, she remained as quiet as a church mouse. He figured the silence had to be killing her. A woman like Beth was used to rattling nonstop, preening for men, or squealing with her friends.

He glanced over his shoulder. She sat slumped in her saddle. Her head lolled, her chin resting on her chest. Her beautiful sable hair slipped from its pins and tumbled around her. Some unidentified emotion tugged at his heart. Just for a moment he indulged himself in looking at her.

Beth Morgan was the most beautiful woman he'd ever seen. He was a man drawn to beautiful things. That was why the countryside moved him so. The texture and color of the various horizons captivated him.

Really it was the thought of limiting himself to only one small corner of the world that made him content to wander. It was why he ended up owning so many different pieces of it.

Seems no matter where he went circumstances were such that he ended up with twice as much as he started with. Just like now, he'd gone to the Morgans to acquire a few mares and ended up brokering a shipping deal between his father and Robert Morgan Sr., gaining four mares, and now the responsibility of taking Beth Morgan as far as she would go. It seemed to Quaid that good fortune could be as much of a curse as a blessing.

He glanced at the sleeping beauty. It was too bad she was a spoiled little twit with no thought for anyone other than herself. Though he fought it, he found himself very attracted to her.

They were coming up on the stream and the horses needed water and a bit of rest. Beth must be half-starved by now. He almost felt sorry for her. Almost. He knew that she had never starved a day in her life. If she was hungry it was her choice. All she had to do was say the word and she could eat.

Maybe she'd rouse from her nap and realize that she was being stubborn. If not, she would by the time they made camp tonight. It was tough to go through a day and a half of solid traveling without a bite to eat. He grinned. Limiting her food was a stroke of genius. The sooner she decided to turn back the sooner he would be free of her.

Still he had to admit that she had surprised him with

all that she had put up with so far. It seemed he had
been wrong about this hothouse flower. She had a little
bit of grit in her after all.

"Whoa," he called, bringing all the animals to a halt.
Beth's beautiful mare stopped with the rest of the
horses and waited patiently. Quaid dismounted and lead
his horse off the road to the edge of the stream. He then
unhitched the mares and did the same with them.
"Hey," he hollered and smacked Beth's leg as he passed
by. "Take care of your animal."

She jerked awake and blinked rapidly. "What?"

"We're at the stream," he said as he led the mares
down to the edge. "Take care of your animal."

He concentrated on his own animals. It was tough.
From the corner of his eye, he saw her stretch, the
movement was long and lazy like a pampered cat. Then
she slid from her saddle. The motion caused the riding
outfit she wore to bunch up tight against her backside.
The brief glimpse of her curves made his mouth water.
He pulled his attention away.

The last thing he needed was to get all woolly-
headed over something that would never be his. He had
too many smarts to get tied up with a gal who didn't
know her own heart. Fickle was not something to hitch
your wagon to. She led her mare down beside his and
let her drink. "Where are we?"

"About a day's ride from the Iowa border. The shade
will start to thin out soon. In two days' time we'll be
traveling on prairie grass."

"Robert said the grasses can grow as much as six feet tall."

"It's like a great sea," Quaid said. "The horizon goes on forever. The wind blows constantly so that the grasses roll like waves."

She looked at him. "Sounds lovely."

"It is in its own way," he said. "You might want to take the saddle off her and brush her down. We'll stop for about an hour and let the animals rest."

"Right." She looked at the saddle and sighed. It was the most pitiful sound he'd ever heard and one that was meant to compel a man to help her.

He had to put on his game face. He knew that she had trouble with the heavy saddle, but if she was going to make it all the way to Wyoming she needed to toughen up.

It was her choice after all. All she had to do was give up and go home. Then he'd take care of everything.

She didn't.

"Come on, Buttercup," she said and pulled her animal to the shade of a nearby tree. Then she went about the long and arduous process of unsaddling her horse.

If nothing else, Quaid had to admire her stubbornness. He had the stallion and four mares down to blankets and rubbed before she managed to yank her saddle to the ground. She sat down on top of it and rested her head in her hands.

It was heartbreaking, really heartbreaking to see her so exhausted. He took a step toward her, but she got up and turned away from him before he went any farther. She crooned to the mare and brushed her with a small curry brush she had packed.

He lounged on the ground and took out a piece of journey cake. She noticed the moment he took it out of its wrapping. Her gaze was drawn to it like a hungry dog to a bone. He heard her stomach rumble. It was loud enough to be heard in the next county and almost made him give in.

"That probably has mealworms in it by now," she said tartly.

"Yum, meat," he countered and took a big bite. She groaned and looked away. This time he didn't hide the grin. He gave her another hour max and she would be begging him to take her home.

She finished with her horse and hobbled her, then wandered away from the small makeshift camp. "Where are you going?"

"Don't worry," she tossed over her shoulder. "If I don't come back you can keep Buttercup."

He wasn't too sure he liked the sound of that. He kept a keen eye on her as she moved into the brush. If she didn't come back in a few minutes, he'd go in after her. She might be a spoiled handful, but he had promised to look after her. He pulled out a small chunk of cheese. He had plenty of both cake and cheese stored away for the moment she gave in. She had to give in pretty soon. Even the toughest pioneer woman had need for solid food.

He washed his lunch down with water from his canteen. It was quiet, too quiet. He got up and followed her path into the brush, his hand on his six-shooter. No sense in trusting that they were alone near this creek. Suddenly he felt stupid for letting her wander off by herself. What if she had gotten into trouble?

A fine sweat crawled down his back. He glanced around. There was no sign of her, except for a broken branch proving she had come through this way. He glanced back at the horses. They munched on grass while swooshing flies with their tails. There couldn't be too much danger nearby; his stallion would have sounded a warning.

He moved farther in and saw that the creek folded back into the wood. He eased along the tree line, stopping long enough to listen. He heard a splash up ahead and took off. He broke out of the woods a few yards away.

He halted at the sight before him. Beth stood knee-deep in the stream. Her hair was in disarray, half of it trailing out of its moorings. Water glistened on her sun-pinkened cheeks. She laughed like a delighted child while a fat trout wiggled inelegantly in her hands.

"What do you think you're doing?" The words came out a bit more demanding than he'd meant them to, but geez, the girl was soaking wet and totally unprotected.

"Look," she said with delight, her sparkling blue eyes smiling. "I caught a fish!"

He pulled his gaze from the happy sparkle in her

eyes and took note that she had hiked her skirts up into her waistband. Not that it mattered—the fish had soaked her from stem to stern.

"So it seems," he said dryly, carefully putting his gun back in his hip holster. He crossed his arms and studied her. "What the heck do you think you're going to do with it?"

"Eat it," she said, the joy rushing out of her face. Haughty disdain took its place and his heart pounded against his chest. He didn't know which was more attractive, her satisfied grin or her challenging look. He held his distance and watched her struggle to wade through the water and not lose her prize.

"You're going to eat it?"

"Yes," she said and wobbled her way through the rapidly running current, struggling against stubbing her toes on the rocky bottom. "I'm starving and I caught it and now I'm going to eat it."

"Raw?"

"No, silly, I'm going to cook it." She nearly slipped and Quaid decided he'd had enough of this silliness. He took two strides into the water and grabbed her, hauling her, fish and all into his arms.

"What do you think you're doing?" she squawked.

"Saving you from drowning." He made his way carefully up the slippery slope of the stream bed.

"I'll have you know I am perfectly capable of swimming."

"I bet you are," he muttered and tried not to think

about how good she felt in his arms, her body tucked up against his. "And I just bet you're stubborn enough not to let go of that darned fish."

"This fish is a very nice trout and you'll be lucky if I offer you a single bite."

"Not a problem. Raw fish is not something I look forward to eating."

"I told you I'm going to cook it. I can cook."

"Right, with what? We're not stopping long enough for a fire."

"Yes we are," she said and put up her chin. The motion was a stubborn challenge that had him ease up. Good lord, if it wasn't for that fish he'd dip his head down and kiss the stubbornness right off her mouth.

She seemed to have read his mind. She slapped the fish against his chest for protection. "Stop right there, mister." She took a deep breath and his gaze went to her damp, trembling bosom. He felt his mouth go dry and glanced back up at her face. He completely forgot what they were talking about and why he was carrying her. The air temperature around them seemed to jump more than ten degrees as he fought an inner battle not to yank that fish out of her hands and show her real hunger.

"Don't you even think about it," she warned and struggled hard in his arms. "Put me down, right now."

"Or, what?" he muttered, his mind mush.

"Or I'll hit you upside the head with this fish."

He laughed then at the absurdity of the whole situation. She blushed a becoming rose color, darkening her sunburn.

"Stop laughing at me," she said, her gaze stormy. "Oh, I could just kill you."

"I think killing me is the last thing you want to do."

"I think you'd better think again," she said, her tone serious enough to have him raising an eyebrow; her fingers still clenching the flopping fish.

This was just ridiculous. He had to pull himself together. He hadn't been this muddle-brained for a woman in years, especially a woman like Beth Morgan. One who had money and means. One who expected nothing less than to be waited on hand and foot. Darn it, that's exactly what he was doing carrying her out of the stream.

He dumped her at the edge of camp. The action was so unexpected that she stumbled and dropped the fish. Gasping she turned to him with eyes flashing thunder and lightning. She swung her arm to slap him, but he caught her wrist before she could touch him. "We're leaving in thirty minutes," he advised her. "I really don't think you want to waste that time beating on me." He let go of her wrist.

"You made me drop my fish. Now look at it. It's covered in dirt." She narrowed her eyes and shot him a look that would have melted steel. "It's going to take me longer to clean it."

"Thirty minutes," he repeated and slammed his hat down on his head.

"I told you, we are not leaving before I get something to eat."

"Better hurry up then, because I'm packing up the mares in twenty-eight minutes. And if I have to pack yours then we're heading back to your father's house."

"You won't have to pack mine," she said in an icy tone that nearly doused the fire in his blood. "I'll be ready."

"See that you are." Then he hightailed it out of there. Distance was a good antidote for racing blood; distance and a long swim in very cold water. Lucky for him the stream was nearby. He'd just have to make sure he swam long enough to freeze out whatever this emotion was she had lit in his veins.

Chapter Four

Beth was so mad she could just spit. The poor fish flopped less and less as it struggled on land. She shook her head at the dirt that coated its sides. "Thirty minutes, indeed," she muttered.

It would take too long to go back to the stream and wash her fish. A sweet thought of revenge entered her brain and she looked around until she spied Quaid's canteen. It hung from a branch on the other side of the camp.

She picked her way through the pine needles and twigs and wished she hadn't thought to remove her shoes before she had gone trout tickling. Her feet were tender. It had been a long time since she had run through the woods barefoot and camped in the trees as a little girl. That didn't mean she couldn't feed herself if she got hungry.

She snagged his canteen and used the water inside to clean off the fish, and then put the fish down on a tuft of clean grass and finished it off. She said a little prayer of thanks to the fish for allowing her to eat.

She needed to make a quick fire. Beth gathered up some twigs and kindling until her arms were full, then realized she didn't have any matches.

Quaid did. She glanced at his saddlebags and looked around. The man was nowhere in sight. Time to see what she could find. She hurried over to his saddle and unhooked the leather latch. Keeping one eye on her surroundings, she dug through the contents.

Inside she found two tins of matches, a can opener, a hunting knife and a tin cup. She took one of the tins of matches, put everything else back in the saddlebag and hurried to the other side of the small camp.

She gathered a handful of rocks to ring the area then built a fire the way her brother had shown her, starting small and adding pieces until it was big enough to cook with. Using the skinning knife she had had the good sense to attach to her belt, she gutted the fish, scaled it, then skewed it on a small branch.

She held the fish over the fire wishing she'd had enough time to make a proper spit. The fish began to cook and the smell had her mouth watering. She kept one eye on the camp for Quaid's return. It was odd that he had disappeared for so very long.

"Probably thinks I'll need help with the fire," she muttered and blew a scraggly hair out of her face. Of course her need to cook the fish took precedence over her need to go back for her stockings and shoes. Unfortunately that left her toes exposed to the hot sun. She could feel them turning pink. At least it gave her petticoats and skirt a chance to dry. "Come on baby, cook," she spoke to the fish as if it would make things happen faster.

She eyed the bundles that Robert's mares carried. She should have taken the time to make a spit. Then she could have gone through more than his saddlebags. She blew at her hair again and her thoughts brightened. If he left her alone once, surely he'd leave her alone again. Next time, she'd be ready to pilfer.

She patted the matches that she'd slipped into the hidden pocket of her petticoat and smiled. As far as she was concerned she was already two up on him. The first was that she knew beyond a doubt that she wasn't going back no matter how horrid he got. The second was that his horrid behavior justified her own in return.

After all, she wouldn't have to pinch anything from him if he'd taken her offer to pay for them. It was his greed, she decided that was the cause of the whole problem. Then just to assuage her conscience, she promised herself that Robert would pay him once they reached Cheyenne. One hundred dollars would more than cover anything she might have to borrow from Quaid.

When the fish began to fall off the stick, she lay a kerchief on a rock and put the fish on top of it. Then she carefully tied the kerchief to keep any flies off her meal and put out the fire.

She didn't have much time left, she was tossing handfuls of dirt to douse out the fire just as Quaid showed back up. One look at him and she stilled.

He'd been swimming and hadn't gotten completely dressed.

She blinked. She should be affronted. Men did not walk around in their undershirts let alone bare-chested. It wasn't proper. Somehow she did not express her indignation out loud. In fact she doubted she'd get any sound out of her mouth. It had gone bone dry at the sight of all that lovely skin.

Quaid must go shirtless a lot because his chest and back were as tan as his face and neck. Long lean muscles, corded and bunched over wide shoulders. He had a sprinkling of hair on his chest and her hands itched to touch it to see if it was soft or crinkly.

There was power there, sleek animal power that spoke of years of hard work and health. His waist narrowed down to the waistband of his pants. At least he had the decency to wear pants. She simply could not explain the strange disappointment in seeing them. His feet were as bare as his chest and just as tanned. He looked like a small boy who ran around half-naked near the swimming hole.

There was one major difference. There was nothing

small about Quaid. He tossed her shoes and stockings at her, then ignored her, and pulled his shirt over his head. Quaid sat down and put on his socks and boots.

Beth felt silly standing there staring, so she went to work covering her feet. "Thank you," she said into the silence.

"For what?"

"For bringing me my shoes," she said and worked the buttons through the holes.

"Time's up," was all Quaid replied.

She glanced up.

"Better saddle up because I expect to be on the road."

"Fine." She didn't like the harshness in his voice. He hadn't even asked about her fish. Well, she wasn't going to tell him either.

She gathered up the kerchief and tucked her precious food supply into her belt. Then she called Buttercup over and hurried to saddle her. By the time she finished packing up she barely had enough time to mount before Quaid moved on down the road.

He was an odd man. He hadn't said two words to her since she'd caught the fish. Maybe he was worried. Maybe it was clear to him that his little plan to make her turn around wasn't going to work. That made her happy.

She pulled the small bundle off her belt and opened it up. The fish was still warm and smelled divine. She took a pinch of the sweet flesh and ate it. It was simply the best fish she had ever had. She glanced up at Quaid's back and a thought flashed into her brain.

With a smile, she kicked Buttercup gently and moved up beside Quaid and his stallion. She rode beside him and feasted on the fish. She made sure she made enough noise that he understood how good that fish was. He had to be hungry. A grown man cannot exist on a handful of jerky and cold corn cake.

"Did you have a nice swim?" she asked between bites.

He grunted his answer. The sound just egged her on. She took another bite, swallowed it, then licked her fingers.

"It's too bad you didn't think to do some fishing. The trout really is good this time of year." She picked off another a piece and popped it into her mouth.

He kept his gaze on the trail ahead. She knew she was getting to him. It was such a lovely feeling.

"Robert says they have some wonderful trout in Wyoming. I can't wait to go fishing there."

He looked at her. "Right, you fish regularly."

"Of course, how do you think I caught this trout?"

"How, exactly, did you catch that fish?"

"I tickled it."

"You tickled it."

"Yes, Pa taught us how to do it. You just move real slow and patient and the trout will slide right up into your hands."

"It will just jump into your hands?" He sounded as if he didn't believe her.

"No, but if you watch and are patient, they will accidentally swim between your hands, especially in the middle of the day when they are slow and napping."

"So, you just picked him up."

"Yep, then I cooked him up. I can cook, you know. Well maybe not as well as my sister Maddie, but I do have a few specialties of my own."

"All care of Mrs. Poole."

"Ah," she exclaimed. "Do you seriously believe I can't cook?"

"Let's put it this way, your father has three daughters and still hired a full-time cook. That right there ought to tell a man something."

"Mrs. Poole is part of the family. She does a whole lot more than cook. My sisters and I cooked all the time."

"All the time?"

"Well, a good bit of the time."

"Well, you'll be cooking in Wyoming, I can guarantee that. There are hardly any women and what women there are have their own cooking to tend too."

"Then it's a good thing I'm going. Robert must be starving if he's living off his own cooking."

"And you're not starving living off yours?" He eyed the fish purposefully.

"This is wonderful," she said. "Granted it would have been better with biscuits, but you gave me neither the time nor the ingredients to cook them."

"You'd better enjoy what you have there," he said, a warning in his tone. "We won't be stopping again until well past nightfall."

"Why are we riding so hard?"

"You wanted to get to Wyoming," he said. "I'm getting you to Wyoming. We've had this discussion. If you're not up to this pace, all you have to do is say so."

"Right." Defeated she backed off and finished her fish in peace. Then she washed her hands with water from her canteen and eyed the packs that sat on the backs of the mares.

He may push her until dark, but sooner or later he'd have to stop if for no other reason than to fill his canteen. When he did, she was going to do a little looking. If she had it her way, she'd be making biscuits by morning.

Quaid was surprised by the little gal's fortitude. From the outset he'd figured she be chatting the whole way. If she wasn't chatting then she'd be complaining. She surprised him. She pretty much kept to herself, except when she needed to stop. Even then she was quick about it.

She was taking all the fun out the trip and the miles were passing far too quickly. If she allowed him to keep up this pace, they'd be at the halfway point in ten days. Then there'd be no turning back.

He frowned. It was difficult enough spending two days with her let alone the idea of a couple of months. He adjusted his seating. Throwing himself headfirst into that stream hadn't helped much and he had wasted good rest time hoping beyond hope that he could wear out the heat in his blood.

He had a bad feeling that it was going to be a long trip. She wasn't making it easy.

He glanced over. It was dark now and he had ridden them through dinner, probably past what the animals were comfortable with. Definitely past what he was comfortable with. If he were truthful with himself, he'd admit that he was afraid of stopping. Afraid of making camp and lying down, knowing she would be sleeping only a few feet away.

A vision of her in his arms, her dress soaked and sticking to her skin flashed into his mind. He shook it off and squared his shoulders. He'd been attracted to women before, he'd be attracted again. This would pass. It always passed.

She could barely keep her seat. Her head bobbed like a puppet on a string and she tipped slightly to the right. His heart squeezed. He muttered something under his breath about sweet stubborn women and made the decision to brave his fear.

Finding a nice pull off sight, he slowed the horses and took them off to a treeless area beside the road. From the look of it, people had camped there before. He could make out a large pit of bare earth for a fire. Quaid stopped his stallion on the other side of the fire ring and dismounted.

He never worried about Beth sleeping. Her docile

mare simply followed behind. He walked over and stroked the beauty's nose. The mare nodded her head when he whispered sweet nothings and reached into his pocket and fed her a sugar cube. Taking a deep breath, he faced his fear.

"We're stopping," he announced. Beth didn't budge. He walked over closer. "I said we're stopping. Time to make camp."

She still didn't move and he felt a little fission of fear run along his spine. Was she all right? Had he driven her too hard? Why the heck didn't she say something? He reached up and touched her leg. "Beth?"

She slipped out of her saddle and right into his arms. He caught her deftly, worry mounting. "Beth?" She snuggled against his shoulder with a sleepy smile.

"Are we there yet?" she whispered.

Astonished at how good she felt against him, he blinked. Her eyes were still closed and she rested like a babe in his arms. It confounded him a bit and tugged at his heart.

He adjusted her in his arms. The sweet scent of violets and woman filled his senses. Her hair tumbled over his arm, the soft dark silk of it made him want to touch it, stroke it. Her skin was soft and flushed from the sun. He pressed his cheek to her forehead. She didn't have a fever. "Beth?"

"Hmmm?" She cuddled right up against him as if it was the most natural thing in the world. He suddenly felt like he was holding a very hot potato. He had to put her down and quick. His temptation was like lightning under his skin. He dropped her feet until they touched the ground. Did she wake up then?

No, she simply draped over him from shoulder to toe. It was the most incredible thing he'd ever felt. He tightened an arm around her waist and for a brief moment pulled her against him. All her rich slender curves snuggled into him like a dream.

Sweat popped up on his forehead. Her hat had slipped down to her back, held on by thin ties. He dipped his head and took a deep whiff of her hair. It smelled like sunshine and madness. It was all he could do not to run his hand up her back and touch the part of her that wasn't guarded by whalebone and hard corset.

She laid her head on his shoulder and sighed. "Eric?"

The word was like a douse of ice cold water. He took a big step back and held her at arm's length. "No, not Eric," he said in a harsh tone. "It's Quaid and you need to wake up. We need to make camp."

Her eyes popped open. "Quaid?"

"Yeah, wake up." He stood her up, pushed her away, and, turning his back on her, headed to his horses. "Take care of your animal. We're up again at dawn."

"Wait, what happened?" she asked and staggered a bit until she got on her feet. "How did I get here?"

"You fell off your horse."

"I fell off my horse?" she started after him. "I've been riding since before I learned to walk. I don't fall off my horse."

"Fine, then next time I won't catch you."

"Catch me?" she sounded indignant. "You didn't catch me. You took advantage of me."

That stopped him in his tracks. He turned slowly on his heel and allowed his anger to show in his gaze. He knew that she saw it because she stopped and took a full step back. He took a step toward her. "I have never taken advantage of a woman in my life." He stood toe to toe with her now.

She raised her chin in defiance. The full moon showcased her beauty in a soft light. He'd have admired it if he weren't so darn angry.

"You had your hands on me and I was asleep," she countered. "That's taking advantage in my book."

Guilt fueled his anger. "Look lady, you are the last person I'd ever take advantage of, and I do not take advantage of unconscious women. I can't believe you would think that." He caught himself waving his arms around and disgusted, dropped them to his side. "We've been alone together for nearly three days and we haven't even started this little journey. If you don't trust me, then say so now and I'll turn this little party around so fast your head will spin. You can be back in your daddy's den complaining about your mistreatment before the end of the week."

"I am not turning around," she said, her tone just as angry as his and twice as stubborn. "You can't make me. I don't care what you try, I'm not going." She slipped a pretty healthy skinning knife off her belt and waved it at him. "My father taught me how to ride and hunt and fish and defend myself. So, I'm not afraid to use this if you make me."

He took a step back, hands in the air and shook his head. "Not a problem. I swear I won't touch you again. That is, not unless you ask me too."

That got her. He could feel the heat on her face from where he stood and had to work at not grinning. "I . . ." she sputtered, "I would never."

"Yeah, maybe that's your whole problem."

"Just what do you mean by that?"

"Nothing," he shrugged and put his hands down.

"Oh you meant something, and you're going to tell me right now."

"Or what?" He rubbed his whiskered chin. The day's worth of growth itched. "What are you going to do? Stab me with that? You'll be turning around then for sure. Ain't no one going to take you to Wyoming and if they say they will, then you'll need a lot more than that sticker to stay safe."

She stared murderously at him. He watched her mind working over what he had to say. He could tell she saw the sense in it. He also saw that she didn't like it much.

"Darn it, I'm tired and half starved. Stop messing with me or I may have to cut you just for the pure pleasure." She turned, slid the knife into her belt and headed toward her mare.

He stood there a moment and watched her in the moonlight. The gal bamboozled him. One minute she was all sweetness and light and the next she was a sassy-mouthed tigress. He rubbed his chin again. Clearly he had underestimated her. He shook his head. It was an extremely rare occurrence when anyone, especially a woman, got past his highly developed sense of things. He took a deep breath and headed for his own horses. He had a lot to think about. Especially how he was going to manage to keep his hands off all that spit and fire.

Beth could not believe the gall of that man. How dare he touch her, hold her against him, and then tell her he didn't mean anything by it. The heat in her cheeks only made her angrier. Humiliated, that's what she felt. Only she knew it wasn't true.

She had been having the most incredible dream. One where she was hauled up against all that lovely muscled flesh that she had witnessed that afternoon. In her dream she enjoyed the tickle in her stomach when she rested her head on that broad, hard shoulder. The strange combination of danger and safety she felt in her dreams had left her trying to get as close as possible to Quaid. He smelled of sun and horse and sweet summer wind with just a hint of salt. She had been so close to tasting that tanned skin when he so rudely woke her.

She nearly fell on her backside when she realized her dream had reflected reality. My goodness, she'd been plastered right up against him. She'd never been that close to a man. Eric had always kept a respectable distance. All her beaus had demanded only soft kisses and slight touches, as if they were afraid of her. All that had left her indifferent to the heat and warmth of a man.

Quaid Blair had changed everything. She blew out a breath and her hair flew away from her face. Buttercup whinnied softly and she stroked her mare's neck.

"It's okay, sweetie," she said. "I won't let him continue to push you so hard." She untied her saddlebags and tossed them to the ground. Then slowly but surely she took the saddle off her mare.

Her arms screamed at the effort and she remembered her father once telling her that the pain was always worse on the day after, but it would soon fade.

They would get strong together, she and Buttercup. They would show that cowboy what they were made of.

Ask him indeed! That would be the day. In fact, while she might dream otherwise, it would be mighty cold in Hades the day she asked that man to touch her.

Chapter Five

Good lord in heaven, something smelled good.

She woke up to find a plate full of pancakes resting beside her. Was that butter dripping down the side? She sat up fast and blinked. She looked around. Quaid was nowhere in sight. A coffee pot sent out fragrant steam as it rested in the ashes of last night's fire.

She didn't wait around to be asked. Beth grabbed the pancakes and ate them with her bare hands. She didn't care how pathetic she looked—she was starving. She got up and filled her cup with coffee and kept a lookout for Quaid while she ate.

"Take care of your animal. The sun's almost up," he said coming up behind her. She jumped and nearly choked on the last big bite of pancake she'd stuffed in her mouth.

"Geez, you startled me," she squeaked out once she could swallow.

He ignored her and went over to pour the last of the coffee in his tin cup. "Be sure and fill your canteen before we go," he advised. "It's going to be a hot one."

"All right," she said confused. She gulped the last of her coffee and took the dishes and her canteen down to the edge of the stream to wash them out. She came back to the camp and handed him the plate. "Thank you."

"For what?"

"For the pancakes."

"I didn't make them for you," he said and took the plate from her and tucked it into one of the packs.

"Oh, but—"

"But nothing," he said and went to check the other packs. "The way I see it, I left them, you ate them. I won't be making that mistake again."

"Oh," she felt the heat of a blush rush up her face. If he hadn't meant for her to eat them, why had he left them right beside her? Of course he'd meant for her to eat them, hadn't he?

"Hurry up," he said behind her. "You're wasting daylight."

"The sun's not even up yet," she argued, still puzzled by the pancakes.

"Will be before you get your mare saddled."

She glanced at the sky. Sure enough it had begun to lighten. Ensuring she gave him no reason to turn them around, she saddled Buttercup faster than ever, then made her way into the bushes. Once she'd finished, she hurried to the stream and washed her hands and face in the cold water.

By this time the sky had lightened enough that she could make out a faint reflection. She was a mess. Her hair drooped, her face was smudged, and her clothing wrinkled. Her heart sank just a little. What she needed was a good night's sleep in a real bed, a bath, and time enough to properly wash her hair.

"Sun's up." Quaid Blair was relentless. She gritted her teeth. He really wanted her to go home.

She knew she wouldn't. She couldn't. If it meant that she would have to arrive in Wyoming looking like a hoyden, then that's what it meant.

She resolved to do whatever it took to meet her goal, even if that meant stealing a man's pancakes with no regrets. She hurried through the woods back to her mare. Mounting quickly, she and Buttercup fell into line behind the long lean cowboy and his string of brood mares.

The day promised to be hot and her skin was already complaining from overexposure to the sun. She clamped her full-brimmed hat on her head and took out her neckerchief. Unfolding it carefully, she tied it over her face to limit the sun's effects.

The heat and sun didn't seem to bother Quaid at all. It was probably why he was such a delicious tan color. He too wore a broad-rimmed hat. It was dusty and had seen better days, but she noted that it shielded his face and neck from the harsh elements.

Having nothing else to do, she eyed him carefully. He sat on a horse as if he were born to the action. His long, lean muscles moved in time with the large, powerful stallion. Quaid's legs were covered with sturdy pants that hung low over thick leather boots. His boots were scuffed and as battered as his hat. It was clear from the whittled heels that he was used to handling horses and working with his hands.

Unlike Eric, she thought. She wondered where that thought came from and realized that she was comparing the two men. Eric had a beauty to him that was near to feminine. He had curly blond hair while Quaid had thick, straight black hair. Eric had long pale lashes and baby blue eyes set in a face that still hinted at youth. Quaid's face, on the other hand, had been chiseled into the sharp angles and planes of a man's. Not nearly as handsome as Eric and yet, more compelling.

She swallowed the thought. She didn't want to be attracted to him. She shouldn't be attracted to him. After all, he'd been perfectly horrible to her, even telling her she'd stolen his pancakes.

So she set about looking for Quaid's physical flaws. When Eric first courted her, she had thought he was the ideal man. He was up with the very fashions of the day. He wore clean, well-tailored clothes. His boots were always immaculate, his neckerchiefs perfectly tied.

Quaid, on the other hand, dressed like a man who wasn't afraid of a bit of hard work. His pants were serviceable. His shirts, while clean, were not made of fine linen. Instead they were as sturdy as the body they covered, capable of handling whatever work had to be done that day.

There was something strangely appealing about that. Quaid didn't wear a vest and or even a bowler hat. He didn't smell of exotic fanciful cologne. Instead he smelled of sunshine, hard work, and an after-scent of bay rum.

Eric's hands had been soft and a tad sweaty. Quaid's, she knew from experience, were large and warm and hard. They were clever and capable of whatever was asked of him. She knew beyond a doubt that Quaid would be there for his wife, even if it meant birthing their child alone.

Eric on the other hand would have passed out at the first sight of blood.

She felt impatience soar through her. In fact, it was the very thought of Eric's lack of spine that made her understand just how close she had come to ruining her entire life.

If anyone was going to be spoiled it was going to be her. The last thing she needed was a spoiled man. Together, she and Eric would have been a complete mess.

She imagined that they would have had to hire someone like Quaid to come in and care for them both.

The thought made her snicker.

He glanced over his shoulder at her. "What?"

"Nothing." But she didn't take the smile off her face. Instead she imagined Eric following behind Quaid pointing out how best to do the work all the while careful not to soil his new boots. Then, after a full hour of pointing and careful stepping, Eric would fall into a chair and demand a good drink and for someone to fan him, while Quaid would continue to see that things were done correctly. She would have fanned Eric, of course, complained of the weather, and watched Quaid from a distance, waiting breathlessly for him to get hot and take his shirt off.

What a fool she had been. Well, Wyoming was a new start. With a new set of rules and new people, surely she could make better choices.

The pancakes in her stomach made her realize how hungry she had been. Maybe he finally understood that she wasn't going to go back. Maybe that's why he'd made her breakfast.

"I want to thank you for those pancakes," she said again, "even if you didn't mean to let me have them. I'd be more than happy to bake you some right nice biscuits for lunch."

He didn't answer.

"I won a blue ribbon for my biscuits. I've been told they are the best in the entire state."

"I bet you have." He eyed her. The look made her shiver. She didn't like the tone of his voice. It was as if she were a child he had to indulge.

"I am not a child and I can make excellent biscuits. Are you going to let me make them for you or not?"

He eyed her. "I thought you didn't have any food supplies."

"I don't."

"Then how are you planning on baking me biscuits?"

"You have enough supplies for both of us," she pointed out.

"I told you I don't intend to share them," he said. "Unless we turn around and head back to your Pa's place."

Why of all the . . . , she fumed. The stubborn man had purposefully left her those pancakes. Surely the food issue had been resolved, hadn't it? Or was his plan simply to tease her with just enough to make her want more? Oh, he was incorrigible!

Pancakes or no pancakes, her stomach still rumbled at the thought of starving.

All she really needed was a cup or so of his flour and a ration of bacon. Surely he didn't carry it in his pocket.

The next time they stopped to water the animals, she would have to be quick. Quick enough to take proper care of Buttercup and then pinch a bit of food from his saddlebags. He'd share whether he wanted to or not.

Quaid knew she was near her breaking point, though he admired how far she had come. She was one determined little thing and he gave her credit for it. He'd given her something to think about when he'd left those pancakes for her. All right, so he hadn't had the heart to starve her out. She might be spoiled, but her stubbornness had gotten under his skin. Heck, he had to admit he kind of admired her determination.

It had been hard to watch her eat those pancakes this morning like a starving person. But heck, if she would just relent, he'd fill her belly for the week it would take for them to get her back home where it was safe.

What the stubborn little wench didn't realize was that things could get really rough on the trail. Rougher than just a little hunger. A body had to think quick and be prepared to handle just about anything.

He tried not to think about how she had looked with that fish wiggling in her hands or how she had felt draped across him. She was softer than he'd imagined and yet resilient enough to prove she was not a regular hothouse flower.

He glanced back. She rode with a confidence any man would admire. A beautiful woman atop a beautiful horse. It was enough to take a man's breath away. He mentally shook himself. It'd break his heart to have to wear her down, but it seemed the only way to knock some sense into her.

He stopped well into the afternoon. There was a creek ahead and he knew the animals needed a good rest. "We'll pull off here for a while," he said, eyeing her. "Be sure your animal is taken care of before you go running off. Oh, and stay out of the water, I don't have the time to make sure you don't drown."

"Ah!" she gasped. "I am a very good swimmer you know."

"Who hasn't eaten properly. You'll pull a muscle. Now do as I say and stay out of the water."

"Fine." She swung down from her perch and he snuck a peek at her. Her clothes pressed against her fine shape for a brief moment. He looked away and glanced at the sky. Okay, a peek was nothing to get worried about. It wasn't like he was falling for her.

He swung down and used the sudden burst of energy to remove the horses' packs, rub them down with sweet grass, and feed them each a sugar cube. He walked over to Beth's mare and grabbed the reins, then fed her a cube. No sense in the horse losing out just because its rider was spoiled and stubborn.

"You're getting better at handling the saddle," he commented as she managed to get it to the ground without too much wobbling about.

"I am perfectly capable of taking care of my animal," she said and blew the straggly hair from her face. "And I'm perfectly capable of taking care of myself. Really, there is a simple solution here. Let me take the train."

"I told you, you can't take the train alone and I won't risk these beautiful animals on one. One crash, one tip, and they could be lost." He patted the mare's nose. She nickered under his touch.

"Of all the stubborn, stupid—" she said striding

toward him, then stopping suddenly. Her face went ghost pale and he knew she was going to faint on him.

"Hell." He rushed over and took her by the arms, gently pulling her to the ground. "Put your head between your knees."

"What?"

He gently pushed on the back of her neck until she was seated with her head between her knees. Guilt assailed him. Okay, so she needed to eat. He glanced around. Maybe this wasn't a bad place to stop for the night. They would have less far to travel when they turned back. "We'll stop here," he said. "You aren't fit enough to continue. We'll rest up tonight, get some food in you, and then we'll turn back tomorrow."

"We are not turning back!" She raised her head and weaved a bit, then quickly put her head back down. "I just need some water."

"You need food and you are not prepared to fend for yourself for the next five hundred miles." He closed his mouth firmly on the issue. "We're turning back."

"You can turn back all you like, but I'm not going to."

He shook his head at her stubbornness. "Up ahead is the Mississippi River. We're going to have to cross that by ferry. You have to be strong enough to watch after your animal and make the crossing."

She looked at him, grit and determination in her gaze. "I am strong enough." She pushed to get up and he pushed her back down.

"Sit, have some water." Something in that look made his heart open up. He could not believe he would say it, but the words came out of his mouth. "We make that crossing and there's no going back."

"I'll make it."

"Fine."

"Fine."

He shook his head and finished rubbing down her horse. If she made it across the river, he'd stop in Dubuque and buy her some supplies. She'd earned them.

Beth waited for a count of ten, then got up. Quaid had moved into the woods and she had anywhere from a few moments to several minutes depending on what he meant to do. She hoped he went for another swim.

But she counted on only a short break. So, she moved swiftly. Keeping her ears open and her eyes half on what she was doing and half on the woods, she systematically went through his saddlebags.

She came across another linen wrapped package and pulled it out. A quick sniff told her it was corn bread. She slipped it into her pocket and hurried back to her spot. Quickly and carefully, she pinched half of the cornbread off, rewrapped the other half and stored it safely in her pocket, then stuffed her mouth with the piece. It was hard and dry and tasted a bit like saddlebag and yet she knew she had to eat if she was going to be strong enough to make that river crossing.

She uncapped her canteen and washed it down with warm water. Wiping her mouth with the back of her hand, she was careful to brush away any crumbs. She heard him coming through the woods behind her, so she closed her eyes.

"Make a fire," he ordered.

She popped her eyes open ready to complain about his commanding tone. The sight of two fat fish had her scrambling. "You went fishing."

"You need to eat," he said. "Now, make a fire. I want to be across the river by nightfall. That doesn't leave us much time for resting."

"Okay." She worked with quick efficient movements until there was a nice snap and pop to the fire. He fashioned a proper spit and put the cleaned fish on them. The sight of the fat trout cooking had her mouth watering and she felt just a bit guilty for stealing from him while he was fishing for her.

"How long is the trip once we cross the Mississippi?" she asked. She picked up a stick and drew squiggles in the dirt.

"It will take roughly two weeks to cross Iowa."

"And then?"

"Then about three weeks across Nebraska and into Wyoming."

"So, I need food for six or eight weeks."

"At best," he said.

She glanced at him. He spread his long lean legs out and rested his head on his saddle. He crossed his arms over his chest and had his hat tipped low over his face. It appeared to all the world that he was napping, but she knew better. She could see the glint of an eye in the shadow of his hat. The man watched her like a cat watches a mouse.

"Good thing I have money," she muttered to herself.

"You can't eat money."

"No, but someone must have a store near that ferry crossing. It would be the perfect place for a supply store. I wager I'll be able to get something there."

He didn't reply and she knew the strength of her confidence. He knew there'd be a store, that's why he wanted her to turn around now. Well, she didn't fall for that now did she?

"Costs ten dollars to cross the river."

"What?"

"I said the ferry crossing costs ten dollars."

"But you can get a train ticket clear to Wyoming for that amount of money."

"You won't."

She bit her bottom lip. She really only had twenty dollars to her name. She had hoped to be able to buy a train ticket somewhere along the way. Not anymore. If she made that ferry crossing and bought supplies, she'd be flat broke. Good gravy, the choices in her life just kept getting better and better.

"I'll be able to pay for my crossing."

"Good."

She turned away from him and poured all her attention on the trout. They began to sizzle slightly from the heat of the fire. She wished she had a little lemon or even tarragon to spice them. Beggars couldn't be choosers, Mrs. Poole always said.

If she stayed on this course of action she'd practically become a beggar. She wasn't sure she had enough money to cover two months worth of supplies.

She blew out a long breath. She'd simply have to be frugal and hope to goodness Robert even recognized her when she reached Wyoming.

The fish filled the gaps left by the half piece of pilfered corn bread and her stomach no longer complained. She felt better than she'd felt in days and her optimism returned. She could do it. She knew she could.

The Mississippi was the widest river she had ever seen. They stopped at the top of a bluff and looked out over the river valley.

Quaid was right. There was no way to cross it on your own. It was a bustling transportation waterway. She spotted ten steamboats and several barges traveling north and south. Small ferryboats propelled by odd steam engines narrowly avoided collision as they traveled east to west across the north and south route. Winding in between were small rafts and fishing boats. From the looks of it you could traverse the river on foot if you walked from one boat deck to another.

"Isn't that a bridge?" she asked pointing to the expansion structure to their south.

"Train bridge," he replied.

"Are there no bridges for wagons?"

"The boatmen hate the bridges, say it runs into their right-of-way."

"Is that so?"

"Runs into the boatman's right to earn money." He started down the side of the bluff and into the busy settlement at the water's edge. Beth could hardly take it all in. She managed to follow Quaid into the thick of things. He seemed to know precisely what dock he wanted and who he would allow to ferry them across.

She caught a heavy set man standing at the corner of the dock eyeing her and the mares alike. She didn't like the feral look in his eye, so she eased her pistol out of her bag. She proceeded to check the cartridge and ensure it was loaded before placing in her lap.

The gesture wasn't lost on the man, and he stepped away, presumably looking for easier prey. Quaid glanced her way. His steady gaze moved from the pistol to her face and he gave one slow nod. Beth sat up straight and kept her wits about her. She saw two men attack a third and take off with his horse. Another man stumbled out of a low-slung shack and fell to the ground stone drunk.

The sun beat down, hot and humid. Insects buzzed unmercifully. The smell of mud, dead fish, coal fire and thick brown river water filled her nostrils. Men shouted various orders and curses at each other while wagons battered by. There was the sound of hammers as cargo boxes were being opened or closed depending on the inspection.

From a second floor window came the call of a working girl, trying to catch the attention of men as they stepped off the boats.

It was the seamiest place she had ever been. She glanced at Quaid who was negotiating with the ferry man. How could he possible think she could come here and be safe, and yet it wasn't safe for her to travel alone in a good clean train coach?

Quaid shook the man's hand and moved over to her. The mares stayed put as he came up beside her. "Take out your money, but do it discreetly. You don't want to flash money around here. Even if it is daylight."

"Right." She carefully opened her bag and dug up her cash. Folding it so that it fit in the palm of her hand, she held out her hand.

He took her hand and lifted it to his lips. The gesture was both bold and romantic and had her heart leaping. His silver gaze made her knees go weak. The heat of his mouth shot through her leather gloves, leaving her wishing she had thought enough to take them off.

He lowered her hand and her empty palm. She was so enthralled by the kiss that she hadn't even noticed him palming her cash. She narrowed her eyes at him and kept her mouth primly closed.

He winked at her and turned back to the boatman.

Better to be thought of as prudish than for him to see

the drool that would surely have come from her slack-jawed response.

"Well done," he said when he came back. She didn't reply, certain that her voice would give away the tumble of emotions caused by the simple gesture of a kiss. He glanced out over the noisy dock. "I've dealt with this man before. He prefers cargo over passengers, but he's careful and he's honest."

"When do we cross?"

"As soon as he gets loaded."

She watched as the man and his mate rolled barrels on the long flat boat. Boxes and crates already stood head high. "Will there be enough room?"

"Just."

She glanced at Quaid.

"We'll have to walk the horses onto the boat and keep them quiet during the crossing. The last thing we want to do is distract the captain."

"Right." She worried her bottom lip with her teeth. The boat didn't look all that sturdy. She glanced at the river. It was wild with commerce, most of which moved north and south.

"Okay, time to board," Quaid said interrupting her thoughts. "Get down and walk her on."

Beth dismounted. Her feet landed in soft mushy mud and she realized that she would have to walk Buttercup onto the boat dock then somehow get her to cross onto the boat—not an easy task.

She took the reins firmly and followed Quaid's lead.

He spoke to the stallion, his hand on the animal's nose. The tones were low and soft and the horse seemed to completely trust his master. Slowly but surely, Quaid talked him up the dock ramp then across the six-inch gap and onto the boat.

He tied the stallion to the rail and came back for the mares. One by one he sweet-talked the mares up the ramp and onto the boat.

Beth's heart pounded in her chest. She was a good horsewoman, but she wasn't sure she was good enough to talk a sensible animal like Buttercup onto the creaking, swaying boat. Heck, she wasn't sure she was good enough to talk her sensible self onto that contraption.

For a brief moment she debated not going. That is until she saw a glint of satisfaction in Quaid's eyes. He raised an eyebrow as if to say the choice was completely hers.

She refused to go back.

The only thing left to do was to go forward. She let her determination lead her. Carefully and with a firm hand, she led Buttercup up the ramp. She kept her hand on her horse, stroking her fine neck, easing her trembling. "Come on, baby, you can do it," she whispered. "*We* can do it."

Chapter Six

Quaid watched her bravely draw her animal onboard the low-slung ferry. It wasn't a typical ferry. Built smaller than most, it had only one smokestack. The front held a small deck, then the engine and control room were neat and compact, set to counterbalance as big a load of goods as the owner could get. The back sat long and flat nearest the water. There was only a small rail to keep things from flying off in bad weather. Not nearly enough for a comfortable trip.

But it was discreet and the captain had always dealt fairly with Quaid in the past. They would not have to watch their backs on board, nor would they have to worry that someone would be waiting to steal the horses on the other side.

Beth looked pale and determined as she hopped onto

the deck and drew her mare forward with the rest. A sudden swell had the deck rolling under their feet. She let out a small yelp and her mare spooked. The animal reared onto her hind legs and pulled on her reins.

Quaid knew a bone deep fear when the mare's hooves came inches from Beth. He leaped to grab the animal's reins and soothe it. Ensuring that he was between Beth and the mare's hooves, he spoke in soft sweet tones and offered her a sugar cube. "You okay?" he asked Beth, not taking his gaze off the animal.

"Sure. Good." She paused, then stepped up beside her mare and stroked the animal's neck. "This deck really rolls. I didn't expect it."

"You have to remain calm or you'll spook the animals. I don't want to lose them in the water."

"Right." She frowned and bit her bottom lip. Her neckerchief was down around her chest and her face had turned a bright pink.

"You're sunburned."

She touched her face and blew out a long sigh. "Stupid hat can't block all the rays."

"You'll get used to the sun by the time we get to Wyoming. It's safe to say you'll be as brown as an Indian."

He expected her to gasp in horror. Instead she laughed. "Now that would be something to write home about. Goodness, Eric would cringe at the thought."

The mention of her ex-fiancé's name made his thoughts turn serious. He had failed to persuade her to forget this nonsense and go home. He finally had to admit that he admired her grit and determination. He had assumed she was a spoiled brat running away from her duty. What he was discovering was that she was a thoughtful, resourceful young woman who wasn't afraid to pinch a piece of corn cake if she had too.

He smiled at the thought. There was a lot to like about Beth Morgan. A lot more than he had seen previously. And a lot more than he had initially assumed. She had struck him as the type who flitted from man to man, her biggest topic of conversation being the latest fashion and whether or not there would be a dance on Friday.

"All aboard," the captain shouted and untied the small gate rail.

"Last chance to go home," Quaid whispered in her ear. "There's no shame in it."

She blew out a breath. "What, and miss the greatest adventure of my life? Please, when I'm old and gray I want something to tell my grandchildren about."

The captain shut the gate and locked it, then he hopped on board and untied the boat from the dock. He slipped past them with a tip of his hat. "Keep your animals still. I won't stop if they scramble off."

Then he made his way to the engine room. The steam engine came to life with a roar and a belch of black smoke. Beth kept tight rein on Buttercup. The mare wanted to back up but Quaid had wedged her firmly between the cargo and the other horses.

"That's a brave girl," Beth soothed. She looked at Quaid. "I have her."

"Be sure that you do, it could get a bit tight and I need to take care of the others." He handed her the reins and their hands touched. He went on impulse and wrapped his hand over hers and squeezed. "You'll do fine as long as you keep your legs under you."

She glanced at him and the look in her eyes went straight to his heart. "Thank you." The tone had him moving away as quickly as possible before he was tempted to wrap more than his hand around her.

The crossing was harrowing. Twice they were knocked about by the wake of a larger boat. Once a huge steamboat sailed right at them, its horns blaring. Beth didn't have time to think about how close it had come. She spent the entire time with her hands on Buttercup, soothing and calming the trembling mare.

She glanced over to see that Quaid had his hands full. His stallion held steady as if he had taken this trip many times before, but the four mares were skittish. They pulled and tugged at their reins. Quaid rolled up his sleeves, exposing long lean muscle that both soothed and controlled the animals.

He moved around the deck with the confidence of a man who had sailor's legs. It seemed he knew just what to do to calm the animals. She made a mental note to ask him about it when and if they reached the other side.

The Mississippi surged around and under them. The water sprayed the deck with the scent of river while the thick coal smoke of the steam engine belched out overhead. The captain seemed to know what he was doing as he zigged and zagged to avoid the other boats.

The ride seemed to take forever. Once when she was a very small girl, her older brother Robert had regaled her with tales of the Mississippi River. How it was more than a mile wide in places and sometimes as deep as the church bell tower. How he was certain that there were monsters lurking in its murky depths.

She glanced out over the breadth of the water and wondered if there were truly monsters in its chocolate depths or if they were merely figments of her imagination. She had heard tails of fish large enough to swallow a man and whirlpools that sucked you down and then refused to spit you back out.

She soothed her hands along her mare's neck and took a deep breath. Today was not the day to let one's imagination run wild. The sun sank low behind the trees that covered the banks to the west and a strange sort of twilight closed in around them, thickening the air. The traffic grew the closer they got to the other side. Boats big and small competed for openings to pull along the docks.

The engines blew out a huge belch of black smoke and slowed to a near stop. She glanced at the shoreline. It was several yards away. Beth looked back at Quaid. "We aren't going to have to swim, are we?"

"Not a chance," he said with a grim expression. "Probably waiting for an open dock."

"Okay." That sounded reasonable. She glanced around. Boats bumped and dipped around them. It would be so easy to pirate a ferry. They were stuck yards off the docks with no way to turn back, no room to turn around. All it would take is for a small quick boat to fly beside them, brigands to board and slash their throats. They were like sitting ducks.

"Nervous?"

Beth jumped nearly out of her skin. Quaid put a hand on her waist to soothe her. "It's almost over," he said, his tone as sweet and low as when he soothed the horses.

She shook her head. "I was just imagining how easy it would be for pirates to board us."

"I suppose that happens."

"It does?" She took a step closer to him. "Do you think there are any about?"

"Some days, but not today."

"Oh . . . well, then . . . good." She took a deep breath to settle her nerves and realized that she practically leaned right into him. All right, so she did lean on him, this time on purpose. He felt safe and warm and solid as a rock in the oddly pitching water. It didn't hurt that he smelled good too.

She would love to bury her nose into his shoulder and hide there like a small child. She blinked and pulled away. How could a dangerous man feel so safe? It must be that the lack of food had gone to her head.

"You okay?"

"Yes, fine." She shifted and leaned on Buttercup instead. "The horses are holding up well in all this madness."

"They're smart animals. Brave beauties. Your father breeds beauties a man would be proud to own."

She glanced over at him. He looked at a spot over her head so she wasn't sure if he was talking about her or the horses. She decided he must be talking about the horses. "That's why we're taking the hard way to Wyoming, isn't it?" she asked. "Because horses like these are few and far between in the West."

"Yes," he said and turned his gaze on her. "They are few and far between and therefore must be protected."

"Don't worry, I'll help you protect them." The engines started up suddenly, causing the boat to lurch. She fell back into his arms. He held her tightly while they sloshed around. Then before she could relish the feeling, he let her go.

In that brief instant she felt her heart start to tumble. Then he was gone. Off to help the stallion. Off to soothe the mares.

Heat rushed to her cheeks. He had come by to soothe her just as he did the animals and for a brief moment she had thought about love. How silly could she be?

The one thing her experience with Eric had taught her was that she didn't know anything about love. How ironic. The girl who had been in love so many times now realized how foolish her notions had been. From the time she was six and Bobby Usher had told her she was the prettiest thing he'd ever laid eyes on, she'd thought love involved flowers and sparkling stars, soft whispers and stolen kisses. Love had been one infatuation after another. One romantic imagining after another.

Now she realized that she would have to think differently if she ever hoped to find real love. Love like Maddie and Amelia had. Love with a man capable of more than admiration.

She glanced at Quaid. He had never once told her she was pretty. Never once romanced her or held her hand and yet, he made her feel things she had never felt before. He tortured her and treated her badly and yet, when it came down to it he was there to soothe and protect her. She knew that he would never leave her in a lurch. He wasn't a man to put himself first. There was no primping, no boasting; only a quiet pride in the capability of his hands and the courage of his heart.

She laughed at herself. How ironic that she may actually lose her heart to the one man who wasn't interested in it.

She blew out a long breath. It was going to be a long trip to Wyoming. She glanced across the water of the Mississippi. She had chosen to take this path and now there was no going back.

She looked ahead as the boat bumped up against the western dock. She knew she didn't want to go back.

Her future was before her. This time she wouldn't turn her back on it, even if heartache loomed ahead of her.

They debarked shortly after they lined up with the dock. The boat captain and Quaid guided her to a street full of shops. She went straight to work and negotiated for supplies. Quaid paid for them and even gave her a few moments to post two letters. One to her father telling him that she was well and that they were in Iowa. The other to Robert letting him know that she and the horses were on their way.

Quaid packed the supplies while she posted the letters. When she came out he was saddled and ready to ride. She glanced at a sign boasting of hot baths then back at Quaid. He looked straight ahead, ignoring her silent plea. She knew better than to ask, so she sighed long and hard and climbed into her saddle.

With a pat on Buttercup's neck, they headed down the streets and out of the city. Dark was nearing and the sounds of evening insects filled her ears, not to mention the fading of the noisy docks, and the occasional rattle of a wagon and the call of the tradesmen.

In comparison, the night air was cool and quiet and soft on her pinkened skin. She hadn't realized how tired she was until they left the noise and energy of the town behind them. Night birds called into an enormous moon and Beth felt her eyelids grow heavy.

She jerked her head up and concentrated on Quaid. He rode on endlessly steady. It seemed he took everything in stride from the pitch of a boat deck to the hours of riding it would take to get to Wyoming. She wondered briefly if anything ever pulled him out of his rut.

"How long are we riding tonight?" she asked.

"Long enough to discourage anyone who thought he liked the look of these horses." He didn't turn toward her, but simply spoke to the spot between the stallion's ears.

She blew out a long slow sigh. He wasn't much on conversation, but if she didn't talk, then she'd fall asleep in her saddle. That was the last thing she wanted. Especially after the other night.

Her thoughts flashed back to waking up in his arms. The solid strength of him against her heart. The appealing scent of sunshine and warmed skin mixed with just a bit of aftershave and leather. He wouldn't wake her up that way again. She'd seen to that herself. Heat of embarrassment flushed over her cheeks.

She trusted him more now and trusted herself less. Funny how that worked. She reached down and patted Buttercup's neck, then pushed her to pull up even beside him. Side by side they walked down the long trail as it wound up sloping hills and down. The moon was brilliant enough to give them a good sense of the road.

Cicadas called out their night song. Birds swooped overhead in the blue-black sky, eating gnats as the stars popped out. Fireflies swooshed up from the tall grass, blinking and mirroring the starlight, calling for their mates.

"Can I ask you a personal question?"

"Hmmm," he answered. She glanced over to see if he had been sleeping. His eyes glittered in the moonlight, as aware as any night predator. It scared her and made her feel safe at the same time.

She ignored the sudden beating of her heart. "How is it you came to have such steady legs on a boat? Were you raised on the lake?"

"My father was a seaman," he said with a shrug. "I grew up on a boat."

"Where about?"

"The coast of Maine."

"Goodness, then how is it that you are so comfortable out here?"

"The prairie is just another form of the sea. It heaves and swells. The winds blow hard and soft. The sky is endless."

"So, it reminds you of home."

"I suppose so."

"Why aren't you a seaman in Maine?"

"Family problems."

"Oh, I'm sorry."

"I'm not. It happened a long time ago." He glanced her way. "I ran off to fight in the war, and once that was done, I knew there was nothing for me back in Maine, so I wandered around the West. Learned a thing or two about the animals and the people."

"Pa says you've got a good head for business. One of the best he's ever worked with."

"That's good to know."

"I'm serious," she said. "So tell me, do you have a place of your own? I imagine a man like you could make a fortune off his own place."

"Money doesn't interest me."

"I see." She wasn't sure that she understood. Money interested every man she ever knew. If money didn't drive him, then what did? "So you enjoy working for other men."

"Not particularly."

"I don't understand."

"Not much to understand. I like wandering, and working like I do allows me the luxury to pick up and move from here to there whenever it strikes my fancy."

"Have you never found a reason to settle in one place?"

"Like what?"

"Like a mountain peak," she said and leaned toward him. "Or a lady?" When that met with silence she pressed on. "Really, haven't you ever just arrived somewhere and known in your heart of hearts that that was your home?" It was what Robert had told her he felt when he first arrived in Wyoming. It was a small part of the reason why she was going to Wyoming. She had a desperate need to look into the heart of the land and find her home.

"I can't say I have," he said. He looked at her and the hairs on her arms stood up on end. "Seen a mountain peak that made me feel like I'm home."

"I suppose that's the sailor in you," she said and leaned back. "You probably have a lady in every port."

He laughed then. It was a rusty sound, as if he didn't use it very often.

"What? Did I say something funny?"

"A lady in every port. You've read too many dime novels."

"Surely there has been a girl or two that you stepped out with."

"One or two," he said and sobered.

"But you never settled down."

"Nope."

"How come?"

"How come you didn't marry that Eric fella?" he shot back.

She cringed at the thought. "Point taken," she said and closed her mouth. Sometimes she pushed too far in a conversation, mainly because she was curious but partly because she never knew when to quit.

The following week they fell into a pattern of stopping late and starting early. Quaid noticed with increasing pride that Beth handled her own animal with growing ease. She woke without complaint and was packed and ready at the break of dawn. He had to admit that his first impression of her had missed the mark. The girl had grit and a simple determination that was as lovely to watch as her face and her figure. Heck, if he were to be honest with himself, he was more than half in love with the gal.

Which was wrong. He knew beyond a doubt that he would never have her. She might be different now that he was the only man on the trail, but he knew that as soon as she hit a town, she'd have every man in three states trailing along behind her. As she had said at her father's house, with so many choices, how could she settle on just one? And Quaid refused to share his history. He also had sense enough not to get involved with a fickle girl who left broken hearts in her wake. He had vowed early on not to ever let love lead him to a life of unhappiness.

"There are clouds rolling in," she said. Her tone was tired. It had been a long afternoon of heat and thickening humidity. The sky changed as quickly as a woman's mood out here. He glanced up.

"Storm's brewing," he conceded. "Let's look for a good place to hunker down."

He scanned the horizon. They were near the Nebraska border and about as far away from anything civilized as a person could get. The hills and valleys of eastern Iowa had flattened out somewhat. Trees grew in the etchings left by dried up streams and half-empty riverbeds. The northwestern sky had turned sick green. The ever present wind whipped up, spawning little dust devils to rise and twirl by.

"Looks like there's a creek bed up a ways. Let's head there."

"Okay."

He took control of the tingle along his skin that told him to run. Running wouldn't do any good when you were heading into a storm like the one brewing up ahead of them. He kicked his mount into a slow soft trot. The animals responded to the scent in the wind and the odd sound of the storm.

Clouds thickened as they approached the creek, giving the sky an eerie twilight. Wind blew so hard that Quaid covered his mouth and nose with his neckerchief. One glance told him that Beth had already done the same.

He nodded his appreciation and concentrated on finding them shelter. Experience taught him that they had to go low and yet, a creek or riverbed could swell at an alarming rate. Many a weary traveler had gotten caught up in the fury of flash floods. Just as a group of trees could provide shelter from battering rains they could at the same time draw deadly lightning.

They approached the creek bed. He put up his hand to slow down their progress and carefully allowed his stallion to pick his way down into the winding creek. What they needed was some sort of shelter that would allow them to stay out of the strength of the wind and yet keep them safe from the ravishes of rain.

Big plops of wetness descended upon the earth around them, scattering on his hat, his shoulders, the stallion's sides.

"Quaid?"

"We need a wider bed," he explained. "Too narrow and a flood could carry us off."

As if to prove his point, the sky opened and a torrent of rain battered them. Quaid pulled his hat down lower to shield his eyes as he sought out the right spot. They followed the creek around a curve. Here it widened. A scrub poplar tree rose up out of the bed, its top capping off a few feet above the rise of the bank.

The bank itself was ten feet tall, blocking the north wind. The rain and wind were furious now, and he knew she would not be able to hear him, so he gestured toward the tree. She nodded, her felt hat drenched, rain soaking the duster she wore.

The air smelled of heat and dust. Filled with angry energy, the storm allowed them to slide under the tree right before it turned ugly. Hail fell from the sky; first pea-sized, and then as thick as his thumb.

Quaid dismounted quickly and hobbled his stallion. The animals would be better off if they were not attached. He pulled a rolled canvas off his saddlebags and threw it over the stallion, then untied the mares.

"Hobble them," he shouted when Beth tapped him on the shoulder. Her own mare was hobbled and stood quietly under the shelter of the tree.

Beth nodded and went to work. The wind picked up, blowing cold and sinister. The hail bounced around them, stinging when it hit, tearing the leaves off the tree. One of the mares whinnied in panic. He pulled it under the tree and ran his hand down its neck, whispering soothing things into the poor animal's ear.

They squeezed under the shelter of the tree, avoiding the largest of the hail. Quaid motioned for Beth to move back against the rock surface of the bank. She pulled out a blanket from her saddle and yanked him under it.

Together they hunkered down, their backs to the rocks. The tree and blanket overhead deflected most of the hail's rage.

Suddenly the rain and hail stopped. It grew eerily quiet. Quaid's heartbeat picked up.

"What is it?" Beth whispered.

"Get as low as you can," Quaid ordered. "Keep that blanket over you." He moved away.

"Where are you going?"

"I want to see exactly what's coming," he explained, his heart in his throat. "I have a feeling it's bad."

She grabbed his arm, her beautiful eyes filled with concern. "Don't leave me."

It was the first time she had said the words. The first time she implored him to care for her. He swallowed the emotion that grew deep inside him. "I'll be right back. Just do as I say and get as low as possible. Keep the blanket over your head."

"Don't leave me, Quaid." She sounded as scared and desperate as he felt.

"You're going to be all right," he said with more bravado than he felt. "I'll be right back."

He slipped out of her reach and scrambled out from under the tree. The horses whinnied and shied, shivering against each other. His instinct was like theirs, to run far and fast from whatever was coming.

Intelligence told him otherwise. Quaid pulled himself up over the bank to see what was out there. In the silence the storm grew like an angry freight train. Then he saw it . . . a prairie elephant—the biggest, ugliest tornado he had ever seen and it was headed right for them.

Chapter Seven

The horses whimpered, breaking Beth's heart. She peeked out of the blanket and noted the brown swirl of water rising up the creek bed. In the eerie silence, she heard Quaid scramble down the bank.

"What is it?" she asked, noting the deep concern etched on his rugged face.

"Get down low," he said and threw himself on her. She grunted as his weight hit her, pushing her into the soft mud of the rising creek bed. Her back was snug up against the hard shale. Before she could get a protest out of her mouth, Quaid tucked her head into his shoulder.

The sound of a freight train roared in her ears. The horses screamed and wind so fierce it stole the air from around them barreled overhead. Something hit them, hard. It seemed to bounce off Quaid driving her deeper into the muck.

Beth held her breath, her heartbeat pounding thick in her ears. She was not afraid. Quaid's solid warmth invaded her. His scent surrounded her, soothing her in the face of the storm. She held on for all she was worth.

The wind snatched at them, stealing the blanket, threatening to pull Quaid out of her arms. She tugged harder, wedging herself into the muck of the corner where the riverbank met the muddy bottom. If the storm was going to take him, then it would have to take her as well for she had wrapped herself around him as if he were a lifeline. Her lifeline.

Instinctively, she held her breath, certain that the wind would rob her of that as well if she but opened her mouth. She counted, hoping that it would blow by before she had to breathe again.

The action reminded her of being a little girl and holding her breath underwater. It was a game she had played with her brothers. A game of who could stay under the longest. She had won the game, not because she had good endurance, but because she was stubborn enough to wait until her brothers all surfaced. Even if it meant that she got a little hazy around the corners of her eyes. The memory made her smile inside.

One thousand five, one thousand six.

It wouldn't be much longer. It couldn't be much longer.

Her brother had once told her of the storms they had in the plains. Of the monster he had called a twister. A wind so wicked it tore the trees right out of the ground and tossed them about. A man could be riding his horse in one county, then after the storm, his body, stripped bare, would be found in the next county miles away.

Robert had told her that though deadly, the twisters moved fast. If one could hold on in a place low enough, it would blow by within seconds. Seconds felt like hours as she squeezed her eyes shut and clung to Quaid.

Then it ended. The air stilled leaving only the ringing in her ears and the banging of her heart. She blew out her breath and gulped in thick air. A gentle rain fell and she blinked. "Quaid?"

He didn't answer. Didn't move. He was still stretched out on top of her, shielding her. For a brief moment she wondered if he was alive, then realized that she could feel his heart beating steadily against hers.

"Quaid?"

Whatever had hit them must have knocked him unconscious, trapping her under him. She pushed at him now. He was heavier than she imagined. His face pale. She glanced over his shoulder to see that the creek was rising fast. Tree branches lay everywhere, stripped of leaves; some still floated down on them, heavy with rain.

She feared it might have been a heavy branch that had hit him. "Quaid, wake up." It was a demand now.

The water reached her feet, seeping into her boots. He didn't budge and she knew she was on her own. Beth used the hard rock at her back as leverage and pushed with her legs and arms until she managed to roll him off her.

He rolled into three-inch water and moaned, but his eyes remained closed. The creek rose at a frighteningly steady rate. She had to get them out of the creek bed and she had to do it fast.

Covered in slick, slimy mud, Beth struggled to her feet and glanced about. The tree that had been their shelter was torn in two. The top half was completely gone, the bottom bright with fresh wood, splinters everywhere.

The horses had scattered in the storm, but had not gone far. She whistled for Buttercup. With some relief, she saw her mare struggle through the rising water toward her. The hobble dragged beside her, half ripped away. The stallion picked his way through the branches and the gray falling rain, arriving at her side first. It ignored her, centering it's concentration on Quaid's still body.

"Good boy," Beth said and eased up to him. "Come on fella, let's see if we can't get out of this mess." The water sloshed up to her boot tops now, its current gathering speed. Quaid was nearly three quarters covered with the brown water and she knew that if she didn't do something soon he would be torn away.

She wedged herself between Quaid's body and the

rising stream. Keeping one hand on the stallion, she searched the saddle for a rope. She couldn't lift him, but maybe she could get the horses to drag him up and out of the creek bed.

The rope was thick and stiff. She was thankful for her leather gloves to save her hands from the rope's rough edges. She tied one end to the pummel of his saddle, then uncurled the rest of the rope. She tried to lift him by the shoulders and ended up herself in the water. She sat down hard. Cold water swirled up to her, but the mud from the bottom worked to her advantage, holding her in place like a suction cup. She used her legs to lift up Quaid's head and shoulders.

Then she ran the rope under his arms and tied it as best she could. The knot was too large and probably too loose but all she had the strength to fashion. Exhausted, breathing heavy and up to her waist in rising flood water, she pulled herself and Quaid up until she was standing and he hung waist high out of the water. With a short whistle and a tug, she managed to convince the stallion to move. The horse stepped cautiously along the creek bed. The rising water suspended Quaid's body just enough that she could pull and tug him over various branches.

Buttercup watched with wide eyes from the other side of the creek. "Go on girl," Beth shouted. "Go on, get out of the creek." Relieved, she watched Buttercup turn and climb up out of the shallow bank.

She could do nothing more than trust the stallion to

find the best way out. The animal was smart and soon found a dip in the bank. With some pulling and tugging, they got Quaid up over the side of the creek and away from the water.

"Whoa, boy," Beth half shouted. The stallion stopped and she knelt beside Quaid. The knot on the rope had tightened from being pulled and soaked with water. There was no way she was going to get it undone. Her fingers hurt and her body shivered.

She pulled her hunting knife out of its sheath and cut the rope as close to the knot as possible. She knew that Quaid would be upset about the mangling of his good rope, but she figured she'd worry about it later.

Once she had him freed from the rope, she checked him for injuries. There was a goose egg–sized knot on the back of his head, but his breathing was good. His pulse was strong and she didn't see any sign of bleeding. Beth rocked back on her heels and blew out a breath. He looked pale as a ghost, but he was alive.

It could have been so much worse.

"No time to dwell on that," she muttered. What she needed to do now was to get them some shelter and get out of her mud-crusted clothes. She was chilled to the bone and figured Quaid had to be as well. It wouldn't do to have one or both of them come down with pneumonia.

She glanced at the sky. The eastern sky was thick and black, but the west was a cool clear blue. In between was a double rainbow. Its crisp clear beauty took her breath away.

"Well, God," she muttered, "I hope that's your promise of no more rain." She stood up and rolled the rope back up, securing it to its place on Quaid's saddle. The end was badly frayed and held a thick ugly knot, but there was nothing to be done about it.

Something bumped her in the back. Beth let out a little squeal. She turned to find Buttercup behind her. The mare took a deep sniff, then snorted. Beth laughed and ran her hand along the animal's fine nose. "I bet I smell a fright," she said. "Well, we'll take care of that in due time." She looked around. "How are you, girl? Are you hurt? Are the other mares about?"

The stallion whinnied and Beth turned to watch the other mares hobble over. They were splattered with mud, but looked none the worse for wear. It seemed Quaid had taken the brunt of the storm.

She took stock of the situation. The blankets that had covered the animals were gone, lost to the wind and the flood water. They were far enough away from the stream that the flood waters would not reach them.

It was a good thing. She glanced at Quaid. There was no way they were going anywhere this night. "Okay, we'll make camp here," Beth said out loud more to comfort herself than for any other reason. She unsaddled Buttercup first. The saddle blanket was warm and three quarters dry, having ridden out the storm under the big leather saddle.

"Perfect," she muttered and unfolded the blanket. Then she covered Quaid with it, tucking him in like a mother tucked in a small child on a cold night. It was the best she could do until she was able to see to the horses and make a fire.

It seemed to take hours, but she worked steadily, unpacking the animals, and rubbing them down with handfuls of tall grass. She found a bag of oats rolled up in a waterproof leather holder and rewarded the horses for their loyalty and patience with her.

Once the animals were tended to and rehobbled for the night, she checked her pistols then ventured off to find wood for a fire. The sun began to set and she knew that they would be prey for animals and Indians alike. Camping at the top of a ridge was never ideal, but it was the best she could do.

Quaid had yet to wake up.

The dying light brought long shadows as she picked up pieces of branches and twigs the storm had left scattered on the ground. She heard an odd noise behind her and turned swiftly, gun in hand.

A very thick, gnarled branch devoid of any leaves fell to the ground. It was as if it had fallen out of nowhere. She glanced around startled, looking for a tree. There were none in sight. She glanced up at the clear sky with wonder. The only thing she could think was that the storm had thrown it up so high it had taken that long to fall back down. "Okay," she said and tucked her gun in her belt. "Never look a gift horse in the mouth."

She piled her twigs and branches near their packs,

then she went back to the large branch. She grabbed it and pulled, working and tugging until it was close to the camp. Then she picked up the small axe Quaid had in his supplies and went to work, hacking the branch into manageable pieces.

As cool darkness fell, she had a fire going, large enough to ward off predators. She stood in front of it exhausted. The heat warmed her chilled skin. Stars popped out above her and she knew it would not rain again tonight. Now that she was no longer working, the air chilled her skin, causing her to shiver.

She knew she had to get out of her mud thickened clothes and get dry. She checked on Quaid. He was still as death, but his heartbeat was strong, his breathing even. She grabbed the biggest pot they had and made her way to the swollen creek. With care, she filled it up and dragged it back to camp.

She knew better than to drink flood water, but that didn't mean she wouldn't bathe in it. She set it to heat. Then she took two of the thin branches and set them in the ground as poles, draping a salvaged blanket between them for a shield.

She stripped out of her clothes. Her riding outfit was a total ruin. She shook her head. There was no way she was going to get all the mud out of it. One sniff and she knew that she wouldn't want to wear it even if she did. It smelled bad, like the thick slimy ooze that had sucked her in and no doubt saved her life when the wind would have stolen her away.

"Be thankful for what you have," she muttered. Maybe she could burn them. She poured the heated water into a smaller bowl and, using a sliver of soap she had purchased in Dubuque, she washed as much of the mud off as she could.

The contrast between warm water and cold air made her skin sensitive. She worked quickly, dumping out the dirty water and refilling it with clean warm water. The final task was to wash her hair.

It worked better if there were two people. She stood up and peered over the blanket. Quaid did not stir. She bit her lip. It was kind of foolish at this point to wish he would wake up and help her with her hair. She laughed at herself.

She had once been so pampered and beautiful. Thank goodness there wasn't a mirror nearby. She shook her head. Quaid had been right. She wasn't cut out for pioneering. It was too late to turn back now. All she could do was the best she could and hope and pray that Quaid woke up before anything worse happened.

She sat back down and washed her hair as best she could. They say that mud is good for the skin. She could only hope it had the same effect on hair.

Quaid dreamed of water. Churning, swirling water that threatened to suck him under. He fought against the current gasping for breath. Suddenly a beautiful mermaid appeared. She smiled at him and dragged him to the surface.

He allowed her to hold him. Her touch soothed and comforted him and he no longer cared if he drowned. No longer fought against the current. Instead he simply floated in her arms, relishing the feeling of belonging; the strange comfort of not being alone.

"Quaid?" the mermaid whispered his name.

"Yeah."

"Wake up."

"I'm awake."

"No, open your eyes."

With great effort he did as the mermaid commanded. He opened his eyes to see her leaning over him, her beautiful face filled with concern. He realized that she was even more beautiful than he first thought.

He reached up to touch her cheek. Her skin was soft and warm and smelled faintly of rosewater. He frowned. Why would a mermaid smell of rosewater?

"Quaid," she said. "Do you know who I am?"

"Mermaid," he managed to get out of his dry throat. He licked his parched lips. "Water."

She put her arm around his shoulders and lifted a canteen to his mouth. He was surrounded by the sweet female scent of her. The heat from her body sent shivers along his skin. He didn't want the water nearly as much as he wanted her.

He drank a bit and then she pulled the canteen away. He closed his eyes for a moment. His head hurt so bad. All he wanted to do was drift back into the sea and hide from the pain.

"Oh, no you don't," the mermaid said. "Stay with me Quaid."

"Cold," he managed to get out then the sweet relief of darkness washed over him. He smiled. The mermaid would keep him safe. All he had to do was cling to her.

Quaid dragged her down on top of him. He did it so fast that she didn't have time to react. Beth braced herself against the cool grass and laid her cheek on his chest. His heartbeat was steady and strong. His breathing deep and slow as if he slept.

Unfortunately his shirt was caked with mud and smelled of the thick mysterious sludge she had unsuccessfully tried to get out of her hair.

She sighed and pulled herself away, brushing off the small amount of dried mud she picked up off his shirt. Quaid moaned, his teeth chattered. The fire blazed nearby, but he was still wearing clothes that were damp and dirty. She blew out a breath and made a decision to strip him. She figured that it wasn't altogether wrong if she did it out of duty.

She pushed a damp lock of hair out of her face and studied his long lean form. Surely he had a change of clothes in his saddlebags. She twisted the lid closed on his canteen and searched through the pile of belongings.

One chambray shirt and a pair of pants made out of denim. They had buttons at the fly. Her eyes grew wide. She hadn't thought about actually touching his fly. Okay, well, she wouldn't worry about that right now.

She turned back to where he lay. It probably

wouldn't hurt if she could wash some of that mud off him. She picked up the pistol and the big cook pot and made her way back down to the stream. The waters had quit rising, but they were still deep and moving fast.

Off to her right something slithered away. She swallowed hard and with one hand on the pistol scooped up more water. Turning, she stopped short at the sight of a pair of eyes.

Fear winged down her spine. Slowly, she lifted the pistol and pointed it at the eyes. "Are you friend or foe?" she asked, not expecting an answer.

In a blink, the eyes were gone. She didn't hear anything move. Her heart beat in her ears and she glanced around. Nothing. Quickly she scrambled back to camp. The horses had moved in closer, but nothing else seemed to disturb the sight.

She set the pot on the fire and with more bravery than she felt, she checked the perimeter of the camp. Nothing stirred. She wished desperately that Quaid would wake up and take the gun and make sure everything was all right.

She glanced over at him. He shivered under the damp blankets. Wishing was foolish at this point. If she didn't take care of him, he could get sicker, maybe even die. Then where would she be? Stuck in the middle of nowhere, unable to cross the swollen creek. All she could do would be to press west and hope she hit a town.

The enormity of it all hit her and tears stung the back

of her eyes. "Stupid," she said and brushed them away. She didn't have time for tears. Self pity had been one of her best games. Now she knew it was a foolish waste of time. "Time to grow up, Morgan," she said to the still air.

Then she went to work. Slipping the pistol into her waist band, she picked up Quaid's dry clothes and placed them nearby. Then she poured the warmed water into the bowl, got out a clean strip of cloth and went to work.

Getting him out of his shirt wasn't easy. It was designed to be pulled over his head. Well, how did one pick up a rather large, well-muscled man and keep him propped up while pulling the shirt over his head?

The best answer was to cut the shirt off. She went to work with her hunting knife. The shirt split in two, exposing quite a bit of lovely male skin, up close and impossibly personal.

She bit her lip. Okay, so he was out cold. He would never know anything other than she cared for him in his hour of need. He shivered and she realized she wasn't helping by staring at him.

Beth grabbed the rag, dipped it in the heated water and went to work. His skin was smooth and pliant over thick muscle. His shoulders were wide and just plain big under her hands. She traced the contour of muscle with the rag and enjoyed a secret thrill of touching something so inherently beautiful.

His chest was V-shaped with enough hair to make it

interesting. She washed down to his waistband in long slow strokes. Caught up in her musings, she nearly jumped out of her skin when he grabbed her wrist.

Her heart in her throat, she glanced over to see him watching her with dull eyes. "You tease me little mermaid," he said. "What is it you want from me?"

"Quaid?" she asked, uncertain that he was all right in the head and more than embarrassed to be caught admiring him. "Are you thirsty?"

"Water. Water nearly killed me."

"Yes, but you're safe now. How is your head?" she said and leaned toward him.

"Hurts," he muttered and closed his eyes. "But you make it all better."

"Well, now I really have no idea what to do to help."

He said something so quietly that she couldn't hear it. She leaned in and put her ear near his mouth. "What?" she whispered.

"You saved me, mermaid," he whispered. "Now I'm yours for life."

"Excuse me?" She sat up in a rush. He didn't repeat his words. Instead he slept. She put her hand on his forehead to check his temperature. It was normal. Thank goodness. The bump on his head must be what was causing him to say such queer things.

He belonged to her.

The very idea made her insides quiver. "Nonsense," she said to the cool night air. "Nonsense." She went back to work and finished toweling him off. Then she lifted him as best she could and tugged the warm flannel of his clean shirt over his head.

He slept through the whole procedure. She glanced down at his damp dirty pants and boots and knew she was only half done.

With trepidation, she threw the blanket over his chest and moved around to his feet. It took some yanking, but she managed to get his boots off. With a sigh she noted that she was now covered with dried slime. There wasn't much to be done about it. He couldn't spend the night in wet boots.

She tugged off his wool socks. His feet were cold and puckered white from prolonged exposure to cold water. She washed them carefully, dried them and rested them in her lap. Rubbing them until his toes showed some color, she hummed to distract herself.

It had to be late. The night wind blew soft. The fire popped and snapped. Somewhere in the distance, coyotes called to each other. She touched the butt of her pistol, happy to have it tucked into her waistband. Then she tugged clean socks onto his feet and put them down.

The only thing left was his pants. She could only pray he had the good sense to wear wool drawers under them. She wouldn't know what her father would say if he knew she was undressing a man. How much more embarrassing would it be if he didn't wear anything under his pants?

She unbuttoned his fly, threw a blanket over his lap,

and went around to his feet. If things were going to be exposed, she wanted to be as far away from them as possible. She grabbed his pant legs and pulled and tugged until they slid down. With one great yank, they came off in her hands.

She studied the pants with a sense of satisfaction and just a bit of terror. She peeked up at his prone body. The blanket held in place. Relief and a touch of disappointment followed.

"All right, let's burn these," she said to no one in particular. Then she tossed the damp mud-encrusted pants onto the fire. It spit and sputtered and for a moment she thought the fire would reject them. Then it leaped in a blaze that scattered sparks around them.

She glanced back at Quaid. He was no longer shivering, which was a good thing. She looked at the clean denim pants that she had folded neatly beside him. How the heck was she going to get those on him?

It was a question that needed further thought. She decided it could wait until after she fixed some dinner. Her stomach rumbled at the idea and she realized that she had been working for hours without any food.

"Not that anyone in their right mind would want to eat smelling like a swamp," she muttered and brushed the wayward hair out of her eyes. She washed her hands, saw that Quaid was well covered, and went to work making biscuits and gravy.

They had been so lucky. The supplies were well wrapped, protected from the wind and the rain. Quaid was a clever man. She had thought his precautions foolish at first, but now she saw the reason behind them, they seemed so simple. It was a lesson well learned. One lesson among many she had learned on the trail with Quaid.

Well, she thought, as she stared at the pan of biscuits cooking on the fire, *I'm getting quite good at all this. Maddie would be shocked.*

It was then she decided she couldn't tell anyone what she was capable of. Then they would expect her to actually work.

She laughed at herself. It was good to know she had the choice to work or not. It was good to know that she was capable of being a field hand, a trail manager, a nurse and a cook. Now she knew for sure she was self-reliant. Until then, she had always doubted her capabilities.

When people took over for her, carrying packages, shooing her away from the stove, she had wondered whether perhaps she was inherently incapable of such actions. Now she realized that was not the case. She was just as competent as her sisters. Just as clever.

She shook her head. Why had it taken her so long to realize the truth?

Chapter Eight

"Water," Quaid croaked out the request. His mouth was as dry as if he'd been chewing on cotton. His throat was sore enough to make the request come out raspy.

His head throbbed with every beat of his heart. He sat up and slowly, cautiously felt his skull. Darn it, he had a lump the size of a fist on the back of his head. His thoughts were fuzzy and he opened his eyes but couldn't really focus.

"Here you go," said a soft gentle female voice.

He allowed her to touch him, put a metal canteen to his lips. The water was metallic tasting, but sweet and cool. He'd have gulped it all down right then if she hadn't pulled it away.

Growling at the interruption, he grabbed her wrist. "More."

"Not right now," she said sternly.

He glared at the fuzzy outline of a female face. "I want more."

"Our good water is limited," she explained. "Let's see if you can keep that down before we waste any more." She successfully pulled the canteen away. With a sigh he dropped his head in his hands. He could have taken the canteen if his head would just let him focus on something other than the pain.

"What happened?"

"There was a bad storm," the woman said. From the sound of her voice she moved out of his reach. "Something hit you on the back of your head. You've been out for half the day."

He tried to focus on something other than the pain and nausea that crept into his stomach. "There was a storm."

"Yes. I believe it was a twister."

"A tornado?"

"Yes."

He struggled to remember. "Where are we?"

"Somewhere in Iowa."

"What are we doing in Iowa?"

"We're on our way to Wyoming, Quaid." She said his name with confidence and he opened his eyes and lifted his head out of his hands. He focused on her face.

She was quite lovely. Long sable hair rippled down her back. Her heart-shaped face had smooth china doll skin, and dark eyes flashed in the light of the campfire. She was the most beautiful woman he had ever seen.

"I'm dreaming."

"No, trust me you are not dreaming."

A memory stirred. She looked so familiar, like the mermaid who had rescued him from the bottom of the sea. "How do you walk?" he couldn't resist asking. He had often wondered as a child how mermaids lived when they were out of water. This one was clearly out of water.

"I have two perfectly good feet," she replied and lifted her skirts enough that he got a glimpse of short boots and shapely calves.

"Not a mermaid," he muttered between the pounding in his head.

"Don't be silly," she said and came to kneel beside him. She touched his forehead with her cool hand. It felt so good that he wanted it to stay there. "No fever," she said and pulled her hand away. "That bump must have you a bit confused. Why ever would you think I was a mermaid?"

"You're too beautiful to be out on the plains alone with a scrounger like me."

"Well." She sat back on her heels and studied him. "I think you just gave me a compliment. You must be sicker than I thought. How do you feel?"

"Pounding in my head," he replied. "Stomach feels twisty."

"I have something for the pain."

"Whiskey?"

"Well, I don't have any of that, but I think there was a small bottle in your stuff. What I have is some headache powder."

She left and returned with a tin cup. He took it and lifted it to his mouth. One swallow and he knew she had poisoned him. He spit out as much as he could. "What the . . ."

"Drink it," she ordered.

"No."

"Drink it and I'll fix you a plate of biscuits and salt pork gravy."

The thought of food had his stomach growling. He wasn't sure if that was a good thing or a bad thing. "No."

"Fine. Drink it and I'll bring you that whiskey. Otherwise you can just lie there in pain for all I care."

"You are a hard woman," he muttered.

"No one's ever called me that before," she said with a satisfied gleam in her eye.

Frowning, he gulped down the bitter brew and struggled not to gag on it. If it was poison then at least death would get rid of the pain.

"Good," she said and took the cup from him. "Here." He looked up to see her holding a small plate. The contents of which were warm and smelled like heaven. "You can be thankful now that I'm not a mermaid. I'm certain all they would feed you is cold fish."

He took the plate and eyed it. "Where's the whiskey?"

"You really are insistent, aren't you?"

"If I'm going to die of poison, then I want to die a happy man."

She sighed long and loud. The force of it brushed past his cheek. It made him grin. Well, a half grin was the best he could do considering the pain he was in.

"Foolish man. If I had poisoned you, why would I waste a perfectly good plate of food on you?"

He glanced at the biscuits; they were golden brown and steaming. "Because the food is poisoned too?"

"If you are so sure, then give me back the plate and I'll eat it myself." She held out her small delicate hand.

He defied the motion and instead pulled the plate closer to him, picked up the fork, and scooped up some of the biscuit. It melted on his tongue. Pain or no pain, he'd just died and gone to heaven.

"Does it taste like poison?"

"Hmmph," he said around a mouthful of biscuit. "It's so bad I'm going to have to eat it all and spare you the pain."

"You're so kind," she said and with a snort went to get his whiskey. He shoveled more into his mouth and watched her walk away. She was lithe and lean and lovely. What the heck was he doing with her? Just watching her walk away did things to him and good lord, she could cook.

Had he been lucky enough to marry such a creature? Why couldn't he remember? He was tempted to shake his head until it cleared but one slight turn of his neck and he knew that was just plain stupid.

She brought him the canteen first. "Drink some more water."

"Bossy thing aren't you?"

"Bossy, spoiled, and completely useless," she said and sat down next to him. "Remember?"

He wished he could remember. He drank a couple of mouthfuls of the cold clean water, then wiped his mouth with the back of his hand. "What did you say your name was again?"

"Beth Morgan, silly. I hope that bump on your head didn't take away all your memory. I'm counting on you to see me to Wyoming."

"Beth Morgan," he rolled the name around on his tongue. With the headache powder and food in his stomach the pain in his head had begun to clear. With clarity came his memory. He remembered Beth Morgan: spoiled, lovely, helpless Beth Morgan. Horrified, he moved to get up. "Good lord, where are the horses?"

She put a hand on his arm. It was warm and firm and shot desire right through him. "They're fine."

"They've got to be stressed by the storm. They needed to be—"

"Unpacked, rubbed down, hobbled, and given a treat of oats," she interrupted. "Just a handful each."

He eyed her. "You did that all by yourself?"

"I had plenty of time while you were passed out stone-cold."

Quaid rubbed his chest and tried to piece things all together. "You built that fire?"

"Sure."

"That's a heck of a fire."

"Well, when branches fell out of a clear blue sky I had to take it as a sign that I could use them to keep us warm." She sat back and hugged her legs. "My father taught me how to build a proper campfire when I was small."

"You changed clothes." He noted that her hair hung free and kinked up in the gentle breeze. She wore a simple cotton blouse, a calico skirt, and a thick leather jacket.

"After you pushed me into the muck I couldn't continue to wear my riding outfit."

"I pushed you into the muck?"

"Yep, jumped right on top of me and wedged us both deep into the stream bed. That's probably what saved our lives when the twister roared overhead."

He suddenly remembered feeling how soft and warm she had been underneath him. Even in his fright he had noticed that she smelled like flowers and woman. "Did I hurt you?"

"Maybe a few bruises," she said and shrugged. "I think you were a bit . . . panicked."

"Hmm." He cleaned off the plate, set it aside and opened the small whiskey bottle. One swig warmed his throat and moved into his stomach. He ran his hand across his chest and realized that he wasn't wearing the clothes he had on earlier. "Is this a new shirt? How—"

"You were shivering in the muck and floodwater clothes, so, I cleaned you up the best I could."

He narrowed his eyes. "You cleaned me up?"

"Yep, just a sponge bath, but enough to warm you and take most of the stink off."

The idea of those lovely hands giving him any kind of bath was something he didn't want to think about. After all, she was all wrong for him. He had to remind himself that the last thing he needed in his life was a spoiled woman. He took a swig of whiskey to block the thought out of his mind.

"I couldn't get your pants on though," she said wistfully.

He spit out the whiskey and choked. "You took my pants off?" His gaze went to the blanket covering him from the waist down.

"Of course! They were wet, cold, and frankly smelly."

He was afraid to look under the blanket. "Where are they now?"

"I burned them," she said and leaned back to study the star-filled sky, "along with your shirt."

"You burned my pants?!"

"Well, it's not like you don't have another pair. See, I found that pair in your bedroll."

"You burned my clothes."

"Mine too. We smelled awful and I kept thinking the stink would surely bring out the predators. Aren't they drawn to the smell of death?"

"You took off my clothes and burned them."

"I cut them off actually," she said. "Except for your boots, of course."

"My boots?" He could barely get the words out of his throat. "Good lord, woman, tell me you didn't burn my boots."

"Of course not, silly. You didn't have another pair."

"Those are the best handmade boots in five states."

"Well, not to worry, I didn't burn them."

His head began to pound again. "What did you do with them?"

"I washed them," she said. "They're drying by the fire now. See?"

He followed where she pointed. There were his boots, tipped over on two sturdy branches with steam wafting off of them. Relief like he hadn't known in some time filled him. He sat back and closed his eyes. "Leather doesn't take well to water."

"I know, but since they were already soaked I figured a bit of soap wouldn't hurt."

There wasn't anything to say to that comment. He tried real hard not to picture her washing his boots in a pot of soapy water. Instead he took a deep breath and concentrated on where they were. The last thing he remembered was throwing her down into the muck of the creek bank.

He frowned but didn't open his eyes.

"If I was passed out, how did we get here?"

"I dragged you out of the creek bed."

"You dragged me out? Why?"

"The creek was flooding rapidly."

"So, you just muscled me out of that eight-foot bank?"

"Not exactly."

"Then what exactly?" She had his whole attention now. What had happened? Had he walked out on his own?

"I called for your stallion. He's a well-trained horse, by the way."

"My horse pulled me out?"

"Well, I managed to get a rope around you, and with the help of your horse and the rising water, we sort of floated you out."

"I see."

"That might be why you kept muttering about a mermaid."

"I don't mutter."

"You told me that I saved your life and now you're all mine."

A fission of something very close to fear shot down his spine and he opened his eyes. "I said nothing of the kind."

"Hmmmm." She tapped her cheek with her delicate finger. "Honor would dictate that you are mine until you save my life." She raised an eyebrow. "I wonder what I could make you do."

He glared at her. He had no idea what she was imagining he would do for her, but he refused to follow after her like a puppy. For goodness sake, that's what all the other men did. If that's what she wanted, then she'd have to want something else because it wasn't happening. "You aren't making me do anything," he said grumpily and took another swig of whiskey.

"Made you forget your headache, didn't I?" she practically laughed at him. Darn it she was right. He felt more like himself. Except he wasn't wearing any pants. Time to remedy that. He moved to stand up.

"What are you doing?" she squeaked and turned her back when he flung the blanket off himself.

"I'm giving in to the call of nature," he said, "and putting on my pants." He was relieved to note that his drawers remained. She did have some sense about her. He grabbed his pants and stalked off to the shadows.

He looked around and noted that she had brought him up well out of reach of the flooded creek. The air, now calm, blew cold and he knew if she hadn't thought to get him in dry clothes he could have suffered far worse than a little skin-exposing embarrassment.

He finished his business and tugged on his pants. His feet felt odd without his boots, but he knew that she was right about that too. The boots had to dry.

He picked his way through the dry prairie grasses, thankful for the socks that muffled the sharp edges. He found the horses as she said, well cared for and hobbled within the safety of the campfire.

"Survived that twister, did you old boy?" he asked as he patted his stallion's proud nose. "Thanks for pulling me out of the stream bank. When we hit the next town I'll get you some sugar cubes."

The stallion answered him with a push against the shoulder. He heard a soft whinny and turned to find Beth's mare Buttercup sniffing his shoulder. "No carrots for you young lady." He ran a hand along her side. "I can't believe you all came out of that unscathed. We were darn lucky."

"Thanks to your quick thinking."

He turned to find Beth leaning against one of the other mares.

"If you hadn't stuffed us all in the bank we wouldn't have survived that storm. How did you know?"

"Instinct," he said with an absent shrug. "How did you know to get out of that stream?"

"Hmmm, I don't know . . . maybe the swiftly rising water?"

"Sarcasm isn't very ladylike, Beth Morgan." He stalked her into the darkness. He was proud to see that she didn't back off. Instead she raised her chin and watched him in the starlight. He could barely make out the twinkle in her eye and he had the sudden and distinct urge to haul her up in his arms and kiss her.

"You did everything right." He whispered the words as he stopped a breath away from her. Her small curvy body radiated heat and smelled like sunshine and flowers. All he had to do was lean a little—just a little—and she'd be flush up against him. The struggle was mighty, but he didn't give in to the urge. He refused to be trapped by a pretty face, no matter what his heart was feeling.

"I did what needed doing, that's it," she said. There was a telltale catch in her voice and he knew that she felt the heat that sparked like lightning between them. Lord, that was some headache powder. He'd never had this kind of reaction to a woman before; the kind of reaction that was at once possessive and protective. He reached up and pulled a stray lock of hair away from her cheek, tucking it behind her ear. The motion allowed him to graze his thumb across her soft creamy cheek. Good lord that girl was temptation.

For right now, he indulged himself. "You are most surprising Beth Morgan," he said. "I wouldn't have thought you capable of coming this far let alone doing all that you did today. Weren't you afraid? I mean just a little bit, being out here all alone in the middle of nowhere, with a passed out cold guide? Most women would have fallen to their knees and cried their eyes out."

"I'm not most women," she said. Her sweet breath caressed his cheek. He allowed himself one more indulgence. He palmed the side of her face. The china-like beauty of her cheekbones was softer than the finest silk. Heat shot through him and he knew he was playing with fire. In his palm was a woman he wanted like he'd never wanted a woman before. She was everything he didn't know he wanted, and everything he swore he'd never have.

"Kiss me, Quaid Blair," she said, her tone soft and serious.

Lord did he want to kiss her, but he knew better. He dropped his hand and took a step away.

She reached out and grabbed a fistful of his shirt, stopping him. He deliberately looked from her fist to her face. "What are you so afraid of?" she asked. "Afraid I'll run crying to my daddy? As far as I can tell he's nowhere in sight."

"You're a lady."

"I see. That's why I was the one who hauled you out of the water, built this camp and saved you from freezing half to death. Seems like this lady deserves at least one kiss out of this."

She let go of his shirt, closed her eyes, and leaned forward. Her sweet cupid mouth was puckered tight. Lord help him, he wanted more than a simple peck. That's what he was afraid of. He was afraid that one taste would lead him to want more, take more. She might have nearly been married but he could guarantee that fiancé of hers never taught her how it really was between a man and a woman. That kind of thing wasn't fashionable. He blew out a long sigh.

She opened one eye and peeked at him. "What are you waiting for?"

"I'm not waiting, I'm—"

He went to take a step back when his stallion bumped him from behind. The motion was so strong that it knocked him into her. He caught her, careful to draw her against him quick enough that they didn't end up on the ground. They teetered together for a moment and he cradled her, struggling to catch his balance.

She clung to him, her head fitting snugly against his shoulder. Right where it ought to be. He was not ever going to gain any balance while he held her and yet he couldn't let go.

"Oh!" she said and looked up at him.

He knew then he was sunk. Dangerous or not he had to kiss her. What the heck, he could always claim he was out of his head from the storm.

He leaned down and captured her gasp. She did not pull away. Instead she wound her arms around his neck and jubilantly kissed him back.

The kiss was everything he'd ever dreamed, filled with hope and longing. It began as the soft touch of one soul seeking another. He drank her in. Her sweet scent filled him. She tasted like home. Her surrender rocked him to the core.

Quaid pulled away, raising his head and yet somehow he couldn't let go of her and walk away. That's what he should have done in the first place, walked away.

The Lovin' Kind   135

"Oh my," she said and stared up at him. He swore he could feel her heart gallop against his. This was not good, not good at all.

He let go of her. The action tore his heart out, but it had to be done. They had come too far to turn back and still had weeks to go. If he didn't stop now she would arrive at her brother's vastly different than when she left home.

"I'm not marrying you," he said as if to ward off the idea. He shoved his hands in his pockets and stared at her.

She blinked and wrapped her arms around her waist. "Well, okay."

He didn't like the sound of her voice. He knew he had hurt her and darn it, he didn't want to hurt her. For goodness sake he loved her.

The thought rocked him. He pushed against his stallion in a poor attempt to ground himself. When exactly had he fallen in love with her? He wiped his face with his hand. "Look, I didn't say that to hurt you."

"Okay."

"I just, well, it's just . . ."

"I understand," she said and turned on her heel. She walked off and the sight of her stabbed his heart. He was not usually so callous. She had to understand.

He went after her. "Beth—"

"I understand," she said, pausing but not looking back at him. "The kiss wasn't what you expected. I understand that. I never expected a proposal."

"Didn't you?" He reached out and spun her around to

face him. "Isn't that what you expected? I mean, men simply take one look at you and fall to their knees."

She shrugged and grasped her jacket closer to her. "That doesn't mean I expected you to."

"Didn't you?" He touched her cheek and felt the moisture of tears. "Honey, just because a man kisses you or finds you appealing to the eye does not mean you should marry him. I thought you had figured that out."

She stepped away from him. "Of course I figured it out." The tone of her voice told him otherwise. "I simply wanted a reward for all my hard work. I didn't expect you to declare undying love."

"Beth—"

"It's probably a good thing that the kiss didn't affect me even in the slightest. It would be difficult to go all the way to Wyoming if you were moon-eyed over me."

"Exactly," he said with a nod. "You've already run from one unfit marriage. I wouldn't want you to fall into another." He dragged his hand through his hair. The motion hurt the goose egg–sized knot on his scalp. He relished in the pain. It made more sense than this conversation.

"Exactly," she said with a strange laugh. "I mean, Eric was far more suitable than you. I don't know why I asked for that kiss. I must be out of my head."

"It's been a long day," he agreed. Why don't you go lie down. I'm fine. I'll watch over the camp and bank the fire."

"Okay. Well, good night then."

"Good night." He stuffed his hands into his pockets and watched her walk off toward the fire.

Once she was safely out of sight he kicked the earth. Pain shot up his leg. Darn it, he forgot he wasn't wearing any boots. He had to be crazy, insane to have taken on the task of taking her to Wyoming. What had he been thinking?

The stallion nudged him in the shoulder looking for treats. He scowled at the animal. "You aren't any help. What do you think you were doing pushing me like that?" He reached up and stroked the stallion's long nose.

"What was I doing kissing her? What am I doing loving her?" he asked the last low. The stallion twitched his ears. Quaid knew the animal was as clueless about love as he was. "The best we can do is ignore the problem and hope that it goes away. Right old boy?"

The horse snorted and deep inside Quaid knew he was right.

Chapter Nine

She could not believe she had begged him for a kiss. Beth buried herself in the bedroll and stared at the fire. She reached up and touched her lips. They were slightly swollen and tingly. Goodness that man could kiss. In all her life she had never been kissed like that.

Her whole system was thrown into shock. It was quite embarrassing really. She had kissed many boys. Why, she was six-years-old when Tommy Sampson gave her her first kiss. It had been a swift peck on the check. She had been surprised then by the power of a kiss and over the years kisses had come and gone. Most of them had been sweet like bonbons. One or two had been just a tad slimy, and she had pushed those boys away. Rejection had never been a problem for her. She was the one who always said yes or no. Men never did.

At least until Quaid Blair. "I won't marry you" echoed through her head. Well, she didn't have any plans on marrying him, either. The man didn't have a kind bone in his body.

But what a nice body he had, even very close and personal it looked good, smelled good, felt good pressed up to hers. Beth blew out a long sigh.

She remembered how he stroked the horses, calming them quickly. How he had calmed her during the river crossing. How he had shielded her with his body during the twister. To be fair, she had to admit—at least to herself—that he did have a kind bone in that magnificent body.

That was the problem and it was a very deep problem. It had only been three weeks since she had run away from one wedding. The last thing she needed was to fall into another.

She shook herself mentally and swore to get a hold of herself. Beth told herself that she merely had feelings for Quaid because they were alone together. If there were other men about she probably wouldn't have noticed Quaid in the least.

Except that she had always noticed Quaid, from the first time he had stepped into her father's kitchen in his dusty boots and equally dusty hat. He had taken off his hat to reveal bright silver blue eyes in a tanned face.

His gaze had moved over her in a slow way that was more breathtaking than humiliating. Then just as simply he had dismissed her, instead asking Mrs. Poole to get her father. When the housekeeper had left to do as he bid, Beth had sat on her stool and watched him, waiting for him to say something lovely. Perhaps something about the way the color of her dress matched the color of her eyes.

He hadn't said a word. Instead he had acted as if she wasn't even in the room. It was the oddest thing a man or boy had ever done in her presence. She was quite used to a simple stare, an awkward acknowledgement and even the suave interest of men.

Quaid simply acted as if he were alone in the room. She had gotten up and moved across the room to get a wooden spoon and stir the pot near the stove. He never even looked her way. She would have believed him blind had he not looked at her so intently the moment he entered the room.

She had frowned and stirred the soup, trying to figure out the puzzle. She had decided to ask him what he thought he was doing when Mrs. Poole came back into the kitchen and escorted him down to Papa's den.

Beth had sat down and watched him walk away. Long lean legs with just enough swagger to show off his confidence. It took three more meetings for him to acknowledge her. And even then she had practically thrown herself against him to catch his attention. Then he had merely put his hands on her forearms, and, careful to keep a large distance between them, he'd stabilized her. "Watch out," was all he had said. No,

"Begging your pardon, Miss." No, "Be careful" or even "Isn't it a lovely day for a trip?"

It was after that that she had set out to antagonize him. Slowly, bit by bit, day by day. He rarely took the bait. Instead he simply acted as if she were a spoiled child that should be ignored or disciplined.

It had been so maddening.

She bit her lip and shook her head. She had been intrigued from the start. Mrs. Quaid Blair. She wondered what Papa would think.

She heard him come into the camp and settle down on his bed roll. He'd put on his boots and covered his face with his hat. The sound of crickets surrounded them. Cicadas called and a firefly flitted close by.

She turned on her back and stared at the stars. Maybe he just didn't like young women. Amelia had told her there were men like that. She took a deep breath. Men who didn't like girls didn't kiss the way Quaid Blair kissed.

"Where do you call home?" she asked, looking up at the night sky. For a moment she didn't think he was going to answer.

"I told you, I'm at home wherever I hang my hat."

"Right. A girl in every port."

"Something like that."

"I don't blame you, I suppose. You have no one to answer to but yourself. No wife to worry about, no kids to discipline."

"About that . . ."

She held her breath and didn't answer. Instead she simply waited for him to say what he meant. The last thing she wanted was to leap to conclusions as readily as her heart leaped when he started. She kept her gaze firmly fixed to Orion's belt.

"It wasn't the kiss. You're a fine kisser."

Well, that was a relief, she thought, but didn't speak.

He pulled the hat off his head and turned on his side. "I'm just not the kind to fall in love and get married."

She let that little idiocy fall flat to the ground. Everyone falls in love. It was only whether they wanted to admit it our not. She knew from watching her brothers that some men found it hard to admit that they were in love, hooked, snookered, head over heels. Quaid was probably just like that.

"Good night, Quaid Blair," was all she said and closed her eyes.

After a long and thought-filled pause he answered back. "Good night, Miss Morgan."

Beth smiled. The way she estimated it they had three weeks to go before they crossed over into Wyoming. In that time one of two things would happen: Either she would fall out of love with him or he would fall into love with her. Either way it was going to be interesting.

For the next week Quaid kept his head low and his hands busy. They crossed into Nebraska with a lot less pomp than when they had crossed the Mississippi. The

Missouri River was wide and busy, but less traveled. This time he felt a sense of calm acceptance in both Beth and the horses. Again they stopped for supplies and he noted that she used her last coins to purchase sugar cubes for the animals.

She was very different than the spoiled beauty he had originally thought she was. Without her fancy clothes, strange hats, and silly frippery, Beth Morgan showed off her kind and compassionate heart and a degree of competence he had never seen in a socialite before.

Her sense of humor warmed his heart. She had taken to telling him stories about her brothers and sisters as they grew up. How she never knew her mother. How the ladies of Boltonville had rallied to wed off both of her sisters.

The stories were warm and funny. He stored them near his heart, knowing that there would be some long cold winter nights ahead when he would find himself alone. Then he could remember her stories and the way her face lit up when she told them.

He tried not to imagine what it would be like waking up next to her every morning for the rest of his life. He couldn't help himself. There wasn't a moment when she wasn't on his mind and in his heart.

Maybe he should just take her, kiss her, make her his own. He looked at her and realized that he would be just another in a long line of men whose hearts Beth had broken. It was clear that love was a game to Beth, played for entertainment. She would soon move on to the next interested man, leaving him in the dust just like she had her fiancé and about ten others in Boltonville. Well, a zebra couldn't lose its stripes and Quaid was too dang smart a man to think otherwise. Quaid shook the thoughts from his head. Let some other man fall into that trap.

"My goodness the prairie goes on and on," she said breaking into his thoughts as they rode side by side. The trail had become indistinguishable in the tall prairie grass.

The locals erected signs to keep the travelers from getting lost. Quaid didn't need the signs. He'd been this way before and knew that you simply followed the setting sun and sooner or later it led to the mountain ranges of the west. When they could see the mountains along the horizon, then they would be in Wyoming. The way he calculated it they had roughly two weeks left.

"There are people who say crossing the prairie is the same as crossing the Atlantic. Weeks of rolling grass instead of rolling waves, punctuated by wild deadly storms and strange beasts."

She smiled at him. "No wonder you are so comfortable out here."

They rode up a small swell and stopped at the top. Before them lay a huge swatch of flattened grass. It came out of the north and moved south.

Beth looked at him with questions in her eyes.

"Buffalo herd," he said. He scanned the southern

horizon and spotted a few straggling black forms. "Have you ever seen a buffalo?"

"Once," she replied. "There was a crazy man who tried to raise them like cattle. He said they would be the next big cash crop."

"What happened?" he asked, his curiosity piqued.

"They simply walked right through his fence and disappeared into the woods. Rumor has it you can see one or two still in the woods if you look close enough."

"And the moral of your story?"

"You can't hem in a wild thing," she said with an odd sort of apologetic tone to her voice. "Even now with the best intentions."

He nodded and sucked his teeth. "Buffalo are pretty darn big animals. He would have had to have a heck of a fence to keep them."

"I didn't say he was a bright man."

"What's he do now?"

"He raises chickens. He has some strange idea that they are healthier for you than other meats."

Quaid snorted in contempt of such a ridiculous idea. They headed down the swell and across the flattened grasses. Halfway across he got the feeling that they were being watched. Quaid wasn't a superstitious man, but he'd had enough experience to know that a man's instinct didn't lie when it told him to watch out.

"Hold up," he said as quietly as possible.

Beth halted her animal and watched him. He twisted

in his seat to get a good look around. They were halfway up a small rise and the sky was a big blue bowl above them. He eyed the horizon and the cracks and crevices.

"What is it?"

"We're being watched."

"All right."

"Most likely Indians," he said and set his jaw. "Probably came upon a group hunting the buffalo."

"Now they're hunting us."

"Probably the horses more than us." He glanced at her. "I won't let them hurt you."

"I know that."

The calm assurance in her voice bolstered his pride. She wasn't going to get hysterical. She trusted him to see them through. She trusted him to take good care of her and he would.

He couldn't see anything but grass. That didn't mean a thing. They needed to find a creek or a grove of scrub trees to hide in. "Keep going," he said in a low tone. "When we get over the rise of this hill, make a sharp turn north. Act as though we planned the turn. We don't want them to know we're aware we're being followed."

"Right," she said with determination. Her chin went up and he knew he had never been more in love with a woman than he was right now. He knew he would die for her.

It was the only time in his life he had felt that way. He'd worry about what that meant later.

They continued up the hill and to his relief, he saw what appeared to be a wandering creek bed running between the next butte. Dust kicked up and grasshoppers leaped away as they passed. The air became thick and strangely silent.

He put his hand on the pistol tucked into his belt. If he had to, he'd cut the mares loose and they would make a run for it. It meant losing some of the finest horses he'd ever seen, but Beth would be safe.

"Stick with me," he said. "We'll try to make the creek. If we can get into the bed, we can cover our tracks with water and hide in the scrub."

She nodded in reply. He saw confidence in her eyes and a wariness to her gaze that told him she was smart enough to know that they were in a predicament.

He picked up the pace just enough to move them along quicker without actually running away. They reached the creek bed and he turned around to survey the scene.

A line of six Indians stood on the rise a few hundred yards behind them. "Time to disappear into thin air," he said. "Dismount."

"What?"

"Dismount," he barked in his command mode. She did as he said and they walked their animals to the creek. She eyed him with curiosity, then looked over her shoulder. He knew that the Indians still stood there. It was an intimidation tactic meant to spook them into a run. "Remain calm. They're trying to intimidate us."

"I am calm," she said with a hitch in her voice, "but the intimidation thing is working."

"That's why they do it."

"May I ask why are we dismounted? They could rush us in a heartbeat."

He didn't have time to explain. He sought out the contours of the low creek bed.

"Lead your horse into the water."

"Great, fine," she muttered and followed his lead. "Let's simply back ourselves into a corner while we're at it and give them the mares on a silver platter."

He ignored her and turned them north in the middle of the creek. They walked quickly and efficiently through the water. He knew that they were most vulnerable right now. He did it on purpose.

Quaid bet that the Indians would not move as long as they could keep them in sight. The next thing was hoping that his luck held as he picked the direction to walk in.

"They're still watching us," she said in a half whisper.

"Good." He pushed the stallion forward. The water was cool as it seeped through his boots. The sun beat down hot and dry on his skin and he felt a fine sheen of sweat building.

A hawk swooped overhead in the cloudless blue sky. Insects buzzed. A meadowlark called. The only other sounds were the splashing of their feet and the beating of his heart.

He could smell the thick ripe scent of grass and mud

and ignored the slight taste of fear in his mouth. "Good." The word came out as the answer to a prayer when the creek made a bend around a rock outcropping.

"Good, what?" she asked glancing over her shoulder. "Can they still see us?"

"No," Quaid said. "Time to use that to our advantage."

"You mean mount up and run like heck."

"I mean double back and wait for them in the brush."

"What? Wait for them? Are you mad?"

"I thought you said you trusted me."

She swallowed visibly. "Right."

"So, mount up."

"Okay."

"Now we'll take off as if we are running like heck." He pushed the stallion out of the water at a dead run. They ran about a hundred yards until he stopped them cold. Then he signaled for her to dismount and they walked their horses back toward the water.

They ducked around the edge of the hill, wandering through pieces of broken slate and gravel until they were just inside the brush. There he untied the horses and placed them a few feet apart in the shadows of the old twisted elms and shivering poplars.

He tucked Beth and her mare up against the slope where the creek made its bend. "Don't make a sound when they come by. I expect they will watch the edge for where we exited and then take off after us. When that happens, slip back around the bend and follow the creek south."

"Okay."

"Anything happens, shoot first and ask questions later." He pressed her pistol into her hand. "You can shoot right?"

"Best as anyone under these circumstances, I guess," she said breathlessly, her hand squeezing around the gun. "What about you?"

"I'm going to do a little distracting."

"Will I see you again?"

He eyed her solemnly. "You can count on it."

"Okay."

There was a slight tremor to her voice and her eyes were wide. What he did next was out of pure instinct. He grabbed her and kissed her hard and sweet, then let her go, pushing her until her back was safely against the wall.

Heart pounding, he grabbed a few branches and covered their trail back. Then he mounted up and headed out away from the creek. At best, he would come back in an hour or so and get the mares. At worst, he would keep the hunting party from harming Beth.

He knew if she followed the creek south she would come upon a town or a railway. Either way he knew she was smart enough to keep herself safe.

Beth's heart was in her throat as she watched him mount and disappear over the hill. He rode like a bat out of hell, urging the animal on with his feet and the ends of the reigns.

She touched her lips. He had kissed her like he'd meant it. The kiss bolstered her own courage because she knew that he would find her. She would be all right.

It grew eerily quiet. The air settled thick and hot around her. She watched a fat spider spin a web in the nearby overgrowth and listened for the sounds of approaching danger.

The mares were also quiet in their hiding spots, as if they knew that their survival depended on their silence. One flicked her back with her tail. The sound was as large and raw as Beth's breathing.

She held her gun to her heart. It was solid reassurance in the stifled heat. She also had her hunting knife in her belt and another slid into her boot. She was nothing if not prepared.

The wind blew suddenly with a short gust that caused a dust devil to lift and dance on the other side of the creek. The trees danced under the blue sky and a soundless motion caught her eye.

Her mouth went dry. An Indian on his pony crept along the creek's outer edge. His keen eyes watched the creek bed and the waving trees overhead.

It was shocking how quiet he and his horse moved as stealthily as a cat after a big fat mouse. Good lord, she was the mouse. She didn't want to think about that right now.

A thin trickle of sweat slid off her forehead and traveled just down her nose, causing it to itch something fierce. But she dare not move and draw attention to herself.

A second silent sentry joined the first. They stopped a few feet away, facing the bank where the mares stood hidden.

Beth realized that Quaid had set up the mares that way on purpose. If they were discovered, she would have time to slip away in the commotion.

The breeze kicked up again and suddenly four more men on horseback stood a few yards away. She remained frozen in the shadows. The grip on her gun tight and ready.

Their faces were painted. Their clothes were simple yet efficient for hunting. It frightened her to realize that she was their prey.

They signaled each other quietly and she knew they were listening. She kept her breathing soft and shallow and prayed that the mares wouldn't stomp, whinny, or flick a fly. A million things could give them away.

She would have held her breath, but she could not predict how long they would stand their listening. The last thing she wanted to do was pass out from holding her breath too long.

A fly buzzed around her face. Some odd insect landed on her cheek. She could feel it crawling toward her mouth. She said a silent prayer as the minutes seemed to stretch like hours.

Then one of the men moved forward, crossing the creek. His horse's steps splashed elegantly. The animal raised its head and for a moment she was afraid he would call to the mares or worse—that they would answer.

When he reached the other side of the bank, the scout did not stop. Instead he continued up the hill, following the path they took when they had run.

He stopped at the top of the hill and gave a yelp that caused her to jump. The rock behind her shifted and a handful of small pebbles slid to her feet. She gazed in horror at them, then back up at the group of hunters.

She was in luck. The yelp had been some sort of signal and her hunters had all set out to cross the creek. The sound of their horses moving in the water muffled the small bits of rock that pooled at her feet.

Her heart beat hard in her chest. Her hand trembled as she clutched her gun and the men drew nearer. She could see them very clearly now. They were not red men at all, but only tanned from the sun. Their black hair was well cared for and shone in the sunlight. They had high cheekbones and proud faces.

Different faces than the men at her home. They moved quietly through the brush and followed the trail up to the top of the hill. Then just as quietly, they disappeared.

Beth blinked to make sure that they had really gone. Then she let out a low slow breath. Her brother Henry had always told her to wait to a slow count of ten before running. Sometimes things had a way of seeming more urgent then they were, he had counseled her. Always give any decision at least a low count of ten.

She stayed where she was and whispered.

"One . . . two . . . three . . . four . . ." An Indian reappeared at the top of the hill. The sight of him left her mouth dry. He glanced back at the stream and the brush.

She knew that if she had not remembered her brother's advice, she would have been in the middle of the stream by now and in plain sight of the hunters. When she saw her brother again, she was going to have to hug him and thank him for saving her life.

Chapter Ten

Quaid raced along the rolling hills as fast as the stallion would go. He tried not to think about leaving Beth behind. It hurt him to think about it. Something deep in his chest pained him and for the first time in years he knew true fear.

He stopped a mile out and doubled back as fast as he went forward. There was no sound. No sign of Indians tracking them. He was tempted to crawl back to the creek, but he knew if his ruse was to work, he didn't have time to satisfy his curiosity.

Instead he turned back, racing even faster along the route. It was his hope that he was making multiple tracks. That it would appear like at least two horses continued along this path.

The stallion enjoyed stretching its legs as Quaid

pushed it up one rolling hill and down another. This time he went a couple more miles out until he came upon a small nearly dry creek. Then he turned back, doubling his track and like a madman raced toward Beth and the Indians who might be tracking him.

When he estimated the distance to be half of what he had done, he stopped and stood up in his stirrups to eye the horizon. For a moment there was no movement and fear shot through him.

If his ruse did not work, then he would have to backtrack and follow after the Indians. He had to know that Beth was all right.

Then he caught a small movement on the horizon. "Yes!" He dismounted and eased his panting lathered horse a few yards away from the trail. Then quickly and quietly, he laid his horse down in the tall grass.

The stallion did not like this trick. In fact Quaid knew he would owe the beast a handful of sugar cubes for this one. The animal snorted his disapproval, but did as Quaid requested. "Good boy," he whispered and stroked the beast's neck.

Together they hid in the tall prairie grass and waited. With any luck at all the Indians would ride right past him. Then he would have to hope they spent the rest of the afternoon following the other creek bed.

It was the only chance he had of saving Beth and the mares.

The wait seemed eternal. The sun heated his back and the ground beneath him. Dust crept into his nostrils. Grass waved around him in the constant ebb and swell of the prairie wind. It smelled rich of ripe grasses and prairie flowers. A bee buzzed around his head. He ignored it and kept his gaze on the horizon.

The hunters moved quickly and quietly along the trail. Their confidence sat on their shoulders like a cloak. Quaid realized that it was their confidence that spooked him most. He counted them—six. Maybe half a hunting party. He hoped that the other half had continued to follow the buffalo. Horses were appealing and very tempting, but he prayed food was more important.

The ground vibrated beneath him as they neared. Their ponies covered the distance with ease. The stallion stirred at the sound and Quaid pulled off his hat and covered the animal's eyes. "Come on, boy, just a little longer." The words were faint but the animal's ear twitched at the sound.

They rode in a column. One man out front first. Then several yards back two sets of two rode abreast of one another. Finally the last man brought up the rear. Quaid watched them ride past. Up and over the next rise. He waited, one hand on the ground. No further vibration. They had not noticed that he'd veered off the path.

Still he waited. It was too easy to be spotted on the open range. The gamble was to be far enough away not to be noticed, but not wait too long that he couldn't beat them back to Beth should they figure out what he'd done at the creek.

Finally after what seemed like a lifetime, he put his

hat on his head, let his horse stand up and shake off the dust. Then he mounted and without looking back, raced toward Beth. All he could do now was pray he'd bought them enough time.

Beth watched the lone Indian stand above the rise for twenty-four long heartbeats. Then he turned and disappeared. Beth did not trust him not to come back. She leaned against the rock and waited. The waiting was driving her mad. So, she noted a shadow off a nearby branch and told herself she could go when it reached her toe. The distance was a mere fraction of an inch. Long enough to help her with her perception of time.

One of the mares sneezed. Beth's heart leaped into her throat. She watched the hilltop. No one came. She glanced at the ground. Finally the shadow had moved. She shook off her fear, tucked the gun into her waistband, and mounted.

Slowly, carefully, she and Buttercup slipped around the bend in the creek, leaving the mares as Quaid had instructed. Then she pushed her horse into the water and encouraged her to go as quickly as she could down the center of the shallow creek.

Dangers lurked in the water, Beth knew that. The shale bottom was slippery. There were holes that could be easily missed and yet, she didn't want to leave a trail.

The sun beat down on her back and she pressed her

hat over her eyes. She squinted at the water, hoping to steer her mare away from any sudden disasters.

They rode up and over one hill, down and up another well past the place she and Quaid had first entered the creek. She reached a spot where the bank had fallen into the creek. It looked relatively new as if some flash flood had swept it away. It was there that Beth decided to come out of the water.

She bent down and patted Buttercup's neck. "Okay, girl," she whispered, "let's ride as fast as we can." She urged her mount forward, following the creek south. The buffalo trail crossed the creek and continued west.

She kept an eye out for any predators following the buffalo. She didn't want anyone, man or beast, to get the idea that she was a weak stray. They hurried past the track and continued in a southern direction.

Beth traveled so hard and so fast that she wondered if she would hit Kansas before nightfall. She hoped not. Then she realized that the trains passed between her and the next state south. That bolstered her a bit. If the creek ran out before she hit a town, she would continue south until she found the train. Surely they would stop and let her on.

Then she realized she had used the last of her money in Omaha. She thought quickly. Fine, she would trade her pistol if she had to. Her father had told her it was as fine a piece as any man's six-shooter.

"Thank goodness Papa had some sense," she muttered. "Well, you wanted adventure, Beth Morgan, and you got it," she told herself and glanced around. The entire world appeared empty except for her and Buttercup.

Occasionally a lazy hawk would circle overhead. But in the heat of the day, nothing stirred. Beth told herself she should be grateful. Some things that stirred were best not thought about.

Quaid eased down the hill to the creek as the sun sank behind him. There were no signs of struggle. No signs that anything was anyway other than how he'd left it. Relief filled him.

The stallion called out and one of the mares replied. The sound was music to Quaid's ears. If the mares were still here, then there was a good chance Beth had made it away safely.

He quickly dismounted and gathered the mares, hitching them back to the stallion. Then he mounted and looked for the spot where Beth had gone back into the water. "Good girl," he said with pride. Then he covered the track and led the horses back into the stream.

With any luck he would come upon Beth before it grew too dark and they would be far enough away for the Indians not to bother them.

Quaid frowned. There was something to be said for safety in numbers. He did some quick calculations in his head. They weren't too far off the major wagon trail. Maybe it would be better to blend into a wagon train for the rest of their journey west.

Right now they were too big a target. The plains were big, but the population was small. Word of two people traveling alone with so many horses would get out by the end of the week. They would be marked by greedy Indians and unscrupulous white men alike.

The sun set too quickly for Beth's piece of mind. She wasn't very happy about being alone. All right, she was down right terrified, but Quaid hadn't reached her . . . yet. It was too dark for her to keep going. Both she and Buttercup were exhausted from the day's stress.

She wanted nothing more than a hot dinner and a warm bed. Neither would be found out on the prairie. She debated making a fire. It would keep her warm and keep away most of the wild critters. It would signal Quaid that she was here but that was also problematic. A fire would also signal her presence to anyone else who was interested.

She bit her bottom lip. Anyone with eyes would see that she was quite alone. Unless she wasn't. Her brothers had taught her how to set up a camp's perimeter to warn for invading guests. She was tired and hungry but the last thing she wanted was to be alone in the dark. So she set to work. Building the camp wouldn't be hard, maintaining it would.

The stars popped out in the thick black sky. The wind

blew around the scrub trees that grew up near the creek and her camp sight. Beth made a small fire and cooked up some beans and biscuits. She figured Quaid would be hungry by the time he found her. She ignored the thought *if he found her* that lurked in the back of her mind.

She tugged her coat around her shoulders and eyed the trip lines that she had placed around the outside edge of her camp. They were tied to the empty can of beans and a tin cup. Nothing would get within twenty feet of her without her knowing it.

It was the best she could do. That along with the mound of grass and leaves she rolled in a blanket and put her hat on top of. If anyone could see her from a distance they would think there were two people in the camp. It wasn't much protection, but it was better than hiding in the dark alone.

With any luck, Quaid would show up soon and all would be well. She boiled some coffee. Personally she preferred a nice cup with cream, but Quaid liked the thick boiled brew black. Wasn't much sense in wishing for cream when she didn't have a cow. When the coffee was done and filling the camp with its rich scent, she poured herself a cup and eased her back against a tree.

She had her pistol within easy reach and the rifle across her lap. All she had to do now was stay awake until Quaid showed up.

She leaned her head back against the rough bark of the tree. The night sounds filled her ears. Cicadas humming, crickets calling. Something splashed in the water a few feet off. She thought of Boltonville. If she had married Eric, she would be home now in a big bed with a newly made mattress and sheets of the finest linen.

Why, she would have a housekeeper, Eric had promised her that. She would have lived like a princess. Fresh from a bath she would ring for the maid to bring her a cup of warm chocolate and her new book.

Eric would come in late from his night at the Mason's. He would have washed, changed into his nightshirt, kissed her softly on the cheek and tumbled into bed beside her.

She would have been warm and cozy and bored half to death. She sighed. Then she imagined living with Quaid. She would be in the kitchen, cooking his favorite dish. He would come in, remove his boots, grab her by the waist and kiss her full on the mouth until her toes curled. Then he would grin down at her and pick up a spoon and try her supper. She would swat him away and demand that he wash up before he got fed.

He'd tell her how wonderful her cooking was, how beautiful she was, and how he couldn't wait to clean up to have both. She would grow warm with pride and burst with love as she pushed him down the hall to clean up. Then she would put the bread in the oven so that it would be warm and toasty when he came down to eat. As she pulled it out of the oven and admired her handiwork, he would come in and simply look at her with that spark in his gaze that tugged at her heart.

"Now there's a sight for sore eyes."

She'd smile and throw herself, bread and all, into his arms. He'd carry her up stairs and show her how much she meant to him. Dinner would be cold by the time they got back to it, but her heart would be warm.

She blew out a long sigh.

"Thanks for keeping the coffee hot."

"You're welcome." Beth sat up straight. Wait a minute, she didn't think that. Sheer terror coursed through her veins. She grabbed the rifle and pointed it straight at the back of the man who was helping himself to her coffee.

"Put the rifle down, Beth," he said and filled his tin cup with the hot brew.

She did as he said. "Quaid?"

"Yep."

"How did you get into the camp?"

"Walked."

"But I have—"

"A very good perimeter set. Yeah, I checked it out." He turned and eyed her as he took a long sip of the coffee. "Who taught you how to do that?"

"My brother, Robert."

"Thank God for that."

She stood up and noticed that her legs were cramped, her back stiff. "I must have fallen asleep. How long was I out?"

"Long enough for me to get into your camp undetected."

She shook her head at the tone of his voice. "Don't you get all disapproving. You are the one who left me." Suddenly angry and embarrassed at her wayward thoughts, she strode up to him while she spoke and shoved a finger against his chest. "So, if my attempts at a safe camp aren't good enough for you, well, then . . . well too darned bad!" She said the last while crossing her arms and stomping her foot.

He blinked at her outrage, then he did the most remarkable thing. He tipped back his head and he laughed. She felt the heat of embarrassment sting her cheeks and went to turn away when he grabbed her by the elbows, dragged her to him, and kissed her full on the mouth.

It was a kiss entirely too similar to the one she had dreamed up just a short time ago. A kiss that warmed her to her toes. Then just as quickly, he set her back on her feet and grinned down at her.

"Oh." She blinked up at him, uncertain what to do about it. The kiss. The feelings that stirred inside her.

"Whose your friend?" he asked, the grin still sparkling in his dark gaze.

"What?" She couldn't seem to think passed the kiss. It was as if he spoke another language.

"Your friend," he said and turned her by the shoulders and pointed at the lump of grass and leaves that rested just outside the circle of firelight.

"Oh, you mean Jeremiah?"

"Yes, I mean Jeremi—who? That's not real is it?"

"Well, of course it isn't real," she said and teased him. "I didn't want to appear all alone in a camp." She went over and poked the blanket with the tip of her booted toe. "Jeremiah and I have had some real good talks, haven't we?" She glanced back at Quaid who drank his coffee and shook his head. "Yes, I know," she said in a conspiratorial voice to the lump's hat. "He is a bit bossy and demanding, but I'm stuck with him."

She let out a loud dramatic sigh and shrugged her shoulders. Quaid's laughter filled the still air and stirred her soul. She turned to him. "Jeremiah says since you're so late in showing up, you get first watch."

"I think I'll take last watch," Quaid said as he hunkered down and filled his plate with warmed beans and biscuits. "Since I'm the only one who hasn't been caught sleeping."

"Well, it was a worth a shot," she said to the dummy and sidled over to Quaid. She sat on the ground beside him and looked around. "How'd you find me?"

"Just as we planned. I went back for the mares, then followed the creek south."

She picked up a stick and drew shapes in the dirt. "Do you think they followed us?"

"I hope not."

She glanced over to see his jaw set as he stared at the fire. "But there's no guarantee."

"Nope." He scooped up the remaining beans and washed them down with the coffee.

"Don't worry," she said and patted his shoulder. "I'll

protect you." The comment was entirely tongue in cheek. He glanced her way and opened his mouth to say something when the tin cup and can banged together.

The sound had them both on their feet, back to back, pistols cocked. "Show yourself or die," Quaid called.

Beth's heart banged in her chest. Her back was warmed by Quaid's strength. She was frightened but reassured by his quiet strength. "You'd better do as he says," she hollered into the darkness. "We're both dead-on shots."

"No harm, I mean no harm," said a man as he walked out of the brush with his hands raised. "My name's John Williams. My missus and I got separated from our wagon train in that last storm. I saw your fire and thought maybe we might know you."

Quaid tucked her behind him and leveled his gun on the man. "Where's the rest of your party?"

"It's just my wife, Harriet, and my kids Emily and Joe. I left them up the hill a few hundred yards." He stood in the circle of light. "Your coffee sure smells good." He glanced at the pot of beans simmering. "We lost most our vitals in the storm. Haven't eaten in a couple of days except for a rabbit or two."

"How do we know you're not lying?" Quaid asked in a deadly tone.

"Pa?" came a little voice.

"Stay hidden, Joe," the older man commanded. "These people ain't our friends . . . yet."

Beth made out the shadow of a young boy. He was

thin with big dark eyes and looked to be all of seven or eight. "We have plenty," Beth said to Quaid.

He glanced down at her then back at the man. "Leave the boy. We'll feed him while you gather up the rest of your family."

The man took his hat off in a motion of submission. "You going west?" he asked. "'Cause I won't be beholden to you if we ain't going the same direction. The way I see it, there's a town about a day or so from here. I'll pick up supplies there if you can wait that long."

"Go get your women. We need the company anyway."

The man looked from Quaid to Beth and then nodded. "Joe, come on out here."

The little boy entered the circle of light. He stood in front of his pa and eyed the pot of beans. He was thin and his clothes were worn at the elbow, but they were clean. It was clear he was cared for even if he was barefoot.

"Joe will stay with you, so's ya don't think we're ambushing y'all. Like I said, our wagon's just up the next hill. You can follow me if ya'd like."

"Pa? Can I have a biscuit?"

The man looked at Beth and she nodded. "Come on Joe, I'll fix you a plate."

"Can I take the plate to Ma?" Joe asked her. "She's hungrier than me, 'cause she gave me and Emily the last of our hardtack."

"There's plenty for everyone," Beth said, her heart in her throat. She knew what it was like to be hungry on the trail. Quaid had shown her that. She looked up at Quaid and he nodded his reassurance.

"Thank you, ma'am," the older man said and put his hat on his head. "You and your man are right fine people."

"Oh, he's n—" She didn't get the words out. Quaid grabbed her around the waist and planted another toe-curling kiss on her.

"I'll be right back," he said with layers of meaning. She figured out real quick that for right now Quaid was her man. Safety in numbers and all that, she thought.

"Be careful," she whispered and pressed her hunting knife into his hand.

He sent her a wink and a smile and disappeared into the night with the stranger. Beth looked down to see little Joe watching her.

"Well, then," she said and composed herself. "Let's get you something to eat. You must be starved."

"Only half starved, ma'am," he said with a quick grin and she noted that he had freckles splashed across his nose. "Pa tells me real starved is when you haven't eaten for almost a month. I ate just the day before yesterday."

"Have you ever been that long without eating?" she asked astounded.

"Naw," he said with a quick grin. "I'm good at trappin'. There's always some fool rabbit or squirrel ready to fall into the soup pot. No worries for us Williamses. We've got the luck of the Irish."

"Right," she said and smiled at him. The luck of the Irish was notorious, although from what she heard it wasn't all that grand.

Chapter Eleven

Quaid kept a wary eye on the couple as they walked their wagon toward the campsite. They had two thin oxen pulling the small wagon and the canvas cover had disappeared leaving only the bare frame of the covered wagon.

John Williams talked a steady stream explaining how they had come from Kentucky and hoped to end up in Oregon, the land of opportunity.

The little girl appeared to be about four or five. She sat on the back of the wagon, hugged her rag doll and watched him with solemn dark eyes. John's wife Harriet looked like she might be all of twenty two. It was clear they didn't have a lot of money when they had set out on their journey. She was bone thin. Her cheekbones were high and sharp under big dark eyes.

Her bonnet was made of chambray and barely covered her face. Her dress, like her daughter's dress, was made of patterned cotton. It was clean but well worn and he bet a month of Sundays that she might have had only one more packed away in a trunk in the back of the wagon.

Pots and pans clanked along the sides. The wagon was dark and half-full of furniture. John noted the direction of Quaid's gaze.

"We had the entire wagon full when we started out, but the weight was a bit much for the cattle, so we got rid of pieces here and there. Bought supplies and such. I'm good with my hands so there's nothing I can't make myself once we git settled. Then that storm stole some of it for itself. I have never seen the like. It just fell out of the sky, scooped the wagon up, dumped out our belongings and tossed it aside, like a small child that's done playing with a toy."

"I take it you weren't in the wagon."

"Got some sense in my head," John said and spat on the ground. "I saw it coming actually, managed to get the kids tucked in a low spot. Let the oxen go free. We were lucky. We only lost our cow." He shook his head. "There were people who lost their lives or worse." He leaned toward Quaid. "Come upon some body parts. The boy an' I buried them." He shook his head and spit. "It's only right to honor the dead." He squinted toward the star-filled sky. "I figure whoever it was is lookin' down at us from heaven. Guiding us, ya know?" He slapped Quaid on the back. "That's how we found you."

"Fortunate for both of us," Quaid agreed. As long as these people were as trustworthy as they looked it wouldn't hurt to have company part of the way to Cheyenne. Not quite as large as a wagon train, but then they wouldn't have to pay a master.

They stopped just outside the perimeter of the camp. Quaid cut the trip line and hollered out to Beth that they were back, while John helped his wife and daughter out of the wagon.

"I made up some more biscuits," Beth said. "So, there's plenty of dinner."

"Pa, I ate three biscuits myself and a plate and a half of beans. They got enough for everyone to eat too."

"We're beholden to ya, mistress," John said and took off his hat. "This here is my Harriet and little Emily."

"How do you do?" Beth asked.

The women nodded but didn't speak. "You must be exhausted. Come on then, wash up and get some dinner. Quaid will help your husband make up some beds."

"Aw, they sleep in the wagon," Joe said. "Pa and I usually take guard duty. Me, I can sleep anywhere— even on my feet if I have too."

Quaid ruffled the boy's hair. "No need for that tonight." He sent Beth a look. "There's enough of us now to keep the camp safe."

"Aw, I can keep watch, really I can. I'm good at it too. Besides, I want to pay ya back for the supper."

"All right," Quaid gave in. He knew what it was like to be poor. Charity was the last thing you wanted or needed. "You keep first watch. See that tree right there?"

"Yeah."

"I bet from the top you'll get a pretty good view of the camp. Why don't you shimmy up there and keep watch. I'll relieve you in a few hours."

"All right!" Joe went running. The grin on his face told Quaid he had done the right thing. Beth gave him a look that did something to his guts. It was a look that told him she was proud of him.

He wasn't sure he needed that, but at the same time it made him stand up a little taller.

"Come on then, let's get some dinner," Beth said and herded the women toward the fire pit and the smells of cooking beans and biscuits.

Quaid glanced around the camp. Nothing moved outside of it. The oxen lowered as John unhitched them and let them wander for the night. The horses stomped at the sight of the thin, mean-looking animals, but soon realized they were dumber than dirt and went back to their own ways.

Quaid smiled. He knew animals well enough to read the horse's expressions. The stallion nudged the mares into line away from the cattle and the strange new scent of the Williams' wagon. Quaid knew he wasn't the only one on watch tonight.

It had been a long day. The days ahead could be longer. He moved into camp and sat down next to Beth. She stitched up the hem of his last shirt. He hadn't even realized she knew about it. Then it dawned on him that she had been managing to watch out after him as much as he watched out after her. It was the reason why his clothes always smelled clean and were in good repair.

Lord, she was the perfect woman. How could he have believed she was spoiled? "Thanks," he said when she bit off the string and put away her needle and thread.

"You're welcome," she replied. Then she folded the shirt and returned it to his bedroll. It was a very nice thing to watch. A comforting thing. A wifely thing.

"You're sleeping with me tonight." He didn't know why he said it like that. Sort of a command. She stopped and studied him for a moment. He wished it wasn't so dark then he could better read her expression. Instead he only got fleeting impressions from the flickering fire light.

"Okay."

"Okay." Relief washed through him. He might have let these people in his camp, but he wouldn't trust them that far. Nope, he needed to keep what was his safe. That included the horses and his woman.

At least his woman for now. Heck, who was he kidding? His woman forever.

He tucked the thought away. It was a dangerous one. It would mean a lot of changes in his life, changes he wasn't sure he was ready to make.

One thing at a time. First they sleep, then they keep going to Wyoming. Only when they arrived in Wyoming would he think about his feelings and what the heck it all meant.

He rolled out their blankets on the opposite side of the camp from the wagon and the Williams family. He took off his hat and boots and sat on the blanket. He watched while Beth fussed with things like brushing her hair and washing her face. It was a very intimate scene. One that he didn't want to share with anyone else, but he knew the sense in traveling in a group. He had hoped to keep a low profile, but now that they had been spotted by scouts, they could no longer travel the prairie alone.

He glanced at the Williamses. John had relieved the boy from his watch and the children were tucked into their blankets. Mrs. Williams lay down beside them. Quaid would take the last watch, ensuring that if they did take the horses and run, they wouldn't get very far.

"They seem like nice people," Beth said as she slipped onto the blanket next to him. He watched as she tossed the blanket over their legs and wiggled her way in beside him.

"I suppose," he managed to get the words out. His entire body had gone on alert the moment she moved in beside him. Her sweet clean scent filled his senses. Her heat was soft and marked him to the bone. He struggled to think of something else, anything else but the fact that she lay beside him in the bed.

He tucked his hands behind his head and stared at the star-filled sky. She put her head on his shoulder and he forgot to breathe.

"Quaid?"

"Hmmm."

"Thank you for saving my life today."

"You're welcome."

In the silence he could hear his heart thundering in his ears. She sighed and rubbed her cheek against his chest. There wasn't a single ounce of seduction in the motion. She rested on him like a small child rested on her father's strength and yet . . . yet, it was so much more to him.

Temptation speared through him. He glanced at the others across the fire and was suddenly glad for their presence. Who knows how much hold he'd have on his senses if they were not there.

Giving in to his need to touch her and hold her close to him, he put his arm around her shoulders and tucked her in firmly beside him. "You should be proud of yourself, Beth Morgan," he murmured into her hair. "Not a whole lot of women could have done what you did today."

She didn't reply and he lifted his head enough to see that she was sound asleep. He shook his head at himself and closed his eyes. He was a fool. The worst part

was he knew he was as foolish as the other men who
followed Beth around like a gaggle of puppies and yet,
he was starting not to care. He reached down and planted a soft kiss on the top of her head and allowed himself to drift off to sleep.

Traveling with the Williamses slowed them down
considerably. It took nearly a week to get to the next
town. Once there the Williamses sold some of the furniture in their wagon and traded for supplies. Beth felt
sorry for them. She would have told thcm to keep all of
the supplies they garnered but Quaid had given her a
look. So she clamped her mouth shut and took the
beans and coffee that they gave her to repay the supplies they had used.

She could tell Quaid itched to be free of them. She
hugged Emily and Joe and said her good-byes. Harriet
had not said much the whole trip and Beth was concerned about the look of dull acceptance in the other
woman's eyes.

"Quaid says there's a wagon train due in through
here in the next week," she said to Harriet. "Are you
going to join it?"

"John says that's best," Harriet replied. "He's got his
heart set on Oregon." The words said so much more.
Beth squeezed Harriet's hands.

"God bless you. I hope you find that piece of heaven."

"Me too."

They both knew the odds weren't on their side. Their

possessions dwindled with every step and they were barely halfway to their destination. Beth reached into her pocket and placed a small folded kerchief in Harriet's hand. "Take care of the children."

She hugged her and turned away. Quaid waited impatiently beside Buttercup. Ever since they hooked up with the Williams family, Quaid had quit treating her like a ranch hand. Now he helped her mount up. She accepted the role change on face value.

It wouldn't do for the family to know that Beth wasn't Quaid's wife. Her reputation was fragile and they both hoped to keep it as clean as possible.

Quaid quickly walked around and climbed up into the stallion's saddle. With a flick of his wrist, he trotted away. Beth did the same, Buttercup now aware that she was to keep abreast of the stallion.

Beth looked back once, long enough to see Harriet open the kerchief, then close it quickly and give a short wave. She thought she saw the woman brush a away a quick tear. Beth knew she had done the right thing.

In the kerchief was her favorite pair of gold earbobs. It would be enough to get Harriet and the children back home if need be.

Beth kept her gaze forward and drew in a deep breath. She had changed so much since the day she ran away from Boltonville and a silly wedding. Before that she would have never parted with earbobs. In fact it had hurt her to give Eric back his ring.

She shook her head. What a silly person she had

been. She glanced at Quaid. Did he see that she had changed? Did he find her attractive? She glanced at her dirty gloves, her dust-coated skirt and realized for the first time the true extent of her change. She must look like a washer woman.

Not that there was anything wrong with washer women. They all seemed to marry and have families even if they were brown from the sun and as tough as a hen too old to lay eggs.

She pushed her hat down lower on her head and felt ridiculous. Of course he didn't find her attractive. How many times had she asked him if he ever thought to settle down? How many times did he have to tell her no?

Why would her gift of earbobs change that? Her heart ached in her chest.

Once again she had been a simple fool. Why did she think that all men must love her? Why did she build stories in her head when nothing had been said? An internal battle played out in Beth's head.

But he kissed me. Only to soothe me. He holds me in his sleep. Only because he is a gentleman and wishes not to tarnish my reputation.

She took a deep breath and raised her chin. Quaid had treated her with nothing but kindness. She wouldn't ruin that with silly thoughts of love and happily ever after. She had to grow up and take him at his word.

Quaid was a man of deep integrity. If she really loved

him, she would keep her heart to herself and give him the freedom to be who he truly was—a wandering man.

"That was a good thing you did back there," Quaid said, drawing her out of her sadness.

"What?"

"Giving her those earbobs. Most women wouldn't have done that."

"It was nothing," she said. "I have five more pairs at home." She shrugged. "Being with the Williamses taught me something about myself."

"What's that?"

"I could never be like Mrs. Williams."

"What do you mean?" he asked and eyed her sideways.

Beth took a deep breath and tried to sound as casual as possible. "She could die out there and for what? Love? I can't imagine ever loving a man enough to give up my life like that." *Just my heart*, she thought, but kept that to herself.

Silence drifted between them. It was cold and hard and awkward. She had given Quaid something to think about. Maybe she should continue in the same vein. "How much longer until we arrive at Robert's?"

"About ten days if we ride hard."

"Thank goodness, I cannot wait to get a nice hot bath and out of this dreadful sun." She blew out a breath. "I had no idea how much I hate traveling." When he didn't comment she pressed on. "I'll probably wait out the year and go back home, maybe move to Chicago. I'm sure I can find plenty of beaus to keep me from being bored."

"I'm sure you can." His reply was monotone. His expression closed off and she winced at the sharp pain in her heart.

"I'll make sure Papa has plenty of stable boys and I'll never have to saddle my own horse again."

"Sounds like you know what you want."

She sent him her most dazzling smile, the whole time her heart cracked and bled in her chest. "Of course I know what I want. I've always known. Ask any one of my brothers or sisters. 'Beth,' they used to say, 'You will settle for nothing less than what you want.'" She took a deep breath. "That's what I realized when I ran away from Eric. I wanted something more than the accountant next door."

"So, you'll sample every man around until you find the one you're certain is the best."

"How could I settle for anything less?"

"Right, how could you."

They lapsed into silence then. Beth knew that she sounded fickle. That her statements might just have destroyed any chance Quaid might have had feelings for her. It was for the better really. She was far too spoiled to spend the rest of her life on the trail like Mrs. Williams and she didn't want Quaid to give up who he was out of some sense of duty.

Chapter Twelve

They reached Wyoming with little to no trouble. The weather had been fine, blue skies, sweet southern wind and shorter waving grass. There was no further sign of Indians. No sign of anyone save for deep wagon tracks cut into the sea of grasses and flowers.

Wyoming was a beautiful land of rolling hills and gradual elevation. The last few days had been the hardest Quaid had ever spent in his life. After leaving the Williamses they returned to separate sides of the campfire to sleep. In his heart he knew it was the right thing.

Beth Morgan was a beautiful but fickle woman. She made it clear that comfort was more important to her than a man's heart. She had seen both the hothouse and the prairie and she chose the hothouse flat out. Not that he blamed her. He just wasn't the hothouse kind of guy.

He tossed a stick into a group of scrub brush with disgust. Still, he couldn't swallow the idea of Beth belonging to anyone else; he didn't care how big the man's house was or how fancy his carriage.

Darn it, she belonged on the prairie with him. Nothing had felt more right than Beth in his arms at night. It made him crazy to watch her across the fire from him now, knowing that in the morning they would arrive at her brother's ranch. This was their last night together. After this she would put on her fancy dresses and turn back into the spoiled little princess she had been when they'd first met.

Beth stood on the other side of the camp and rubbed her back with a soft sigh. "Goodness, it will be nice to sleep in a real bed tomorrow."

"I'm sure your brother will have one specially stuffed with only goose down, just for you, Princess."

She blinked and stared at him. "I'm sure he will." He winced at the odd sound of pain in her voice. "Robert takes good care of people. I'm sure he'll have a soft bed for you as well."

"That won't be necessary," he said as he paced like a panther. "I won't be staying."

"You won't be staying? Not even for one night?"

What was the sense in staying and seeing her begin her return to the pampered life? Not out on the trail and in his arms, but safely ensconced in a big house wearing silks and taking gentlemen callers.

"No sense in wearing out my welcome," Quaid nearly growled. "Like I said, I'm a wandering man. I'll just be seeing you home and then leaving."

"So, you'll simply drop me off and leave."

"Yep."

"Just like that. Without so much as a good-bye, glad to know you?"

"Yep." He didn't budge when the comment caused her to flinch.

"Where will you go?" she asked, working the kinks out of her shoulders to hide her distress.

"Not sure," he said with a shrug. "I've got some things to attend to in Wyoming. Then I'll probably wander south."

"Because you're the wandering kind of man," she said with a strange edge to her voice.

"Yep," he said to goad her. "Like John Williams, I like to chase a dream." He thought he saw her wince, and regretted his words. Truth was he owned a sizable spread near her brother. He simply hadn't had any reason to stay at any of his properties for very long.

"So, this is our last night together."

He stopped his pacing and stood as still as a man could get so as not to spook her. "Yeah, it looks like it is."

She sat down and untied the braid from her hair. She took out her big brush and began to brush it. The firelight snapped and crackled along the length of it. He remembered how soft it was. How silky and intimate against his skin when he held her at night.

"Odd isn't it," she said breaking the silence.

He sat down with his back against his saddle and pulled out his knife. "What?" He selected a nice stick and commenced to whittle it. It kept his hands busy and his mind free.

She shrugged and flipped her hair over her shoulder, then brushed the other side. "That we made it this far without killing each other."

"Just proves I'm a man of great patience," he replied, playing the game.

"No it doesn't," she said and put down her brush. "It proves I'm a determined gal."

They both laughed at the absurdity of the situation. She got up and unrolled her bedroll. Her hair spread out around her shoulders, falling in a thick sensuous veil. "Well, good night, Quaid Blair."

She looked so appealing in the firelight. Her beautiful face sincere and for a moment he thought he saw longing, maybe even love. Then he realized it was probably exhaustion.

Quaid blew out a long slow breath. "Come here."

"What?" Beth stood at the edge of her bedroll and eyed Quaid's long legs and sprawled out form.

"I said come here."

"Why?"

"Come here and find out."

She hesitated only a second then went and sat down beside him on his blanket. He tossed the other blanket over her legs and put his arm around her shoulder drawing her up against the hard length of him. She rested her head against his chest and for a moment wallowed in the pleasure it gave her. The wonderful, lovely sense of belonging that she had never found anywhere else.

"Now," he said. "Tell me what you want."

"What I want?" A small fission of fear went through her. "What do you mean?"

"I mean tell me what you see in your future. What you want for your life—now . . . later."

She thought about it a moment. What she wanted was what she had right now this very minute. Quaid all to herself. "I suppose I want a home of my own like my sisters."

"And that guy, Eric, couldn't give that to you?"

Beth chuckled. "Poor Eric. Yes, I suppose he could have given it to me, but I didn't want him as much as I wanted a comfortable place of my own where I can ride horses, grow flowers, and have children."

"So, you really plan on carrying on with every man in Chicago until you find the one you want?"

"What? Oh." She shrugged and decided that honesty was best. "I made that up."

"I see."

She looked up into his starkly handsome face. "Do you see?"

"You said you couldn't understand loving a man enough to live a life on the trail with him. Makes me wonder if you have any idea what real love is."

"I know what real love is."

"Really? What if a man was to have a small ranch

with a log house and a barn? Would that be enough for you? Would you be happy working the land and living through bad weather, bad luck, and not enough food?"

"Goodness, sounds like you are asking me if I would live like I have on this trip."

"Would you? Would you even consider loving a man like that?"

She studied the night sky and tried to be honest. "You've ruined me, you know."

He stiffened under her and she shook her head and patted his chest. "Not like that. I'm certain my reputation is still good," she said and he relaxed. She stacked her hands on his chest and rested her chin on it so that she could see his face. "I used to think the best things in life were baubles and parties and new dresses, but this trip showed me something else. It showed me that I can do things for myself. I guess I learned there is satisfaction in accomplishing things. At the same time, I can't see myself being as dully accepting about things as Mrs. Williams."

He laughed at that and the vibration against her chest made her smile. "No, somehow I can't see that either."

She sat up. "I don't know, I guess life takes you places you never imagined you'd go. I mean look at me now. My hands are a wreck." She studied her trail-roughened hands.

He reached up and stroked her soft hair. "Your hair isn't any worse for wear."

She pulled back until he couldn't touch her. It disquieted her the way he touched her as if she were made of gold. As if she were the most precious thing he had ever seen. She busied herself braiding her hair. "I'm sure it's simply hideous right now."

He reached up and stroked her cheek. "You are far from hideous, Beth Morgan. You'll see that when we get to town. Why, every man within a hundred miles will be swarming your brother's ranch. I'm sure you'll have plenty to choose from while you're searching for real love."

She blew out a breath and tied off her braid with a piece of ribbon. "I'm not interested in a swarm of men."

"Hmmm, you used to be."

"I've changed."

"Really?"

"Really!"

"What are you interested in now?"

"I'm interested in you." Her heart banged in her chest and she met his gaze bravely. "Oh, Quaid, I don't care if you're poor as a church mouse. I love you, Quaid Blair."

He stilled like a rabbit caught in a hunter's sights. The idea hurt her more than she thought it could.

"Beth—"

She reached out and touched her finger to his mouth. "It's okay." She blinked back the pain and sent him a watery smile. "I overstepped myself."

"Don't do this," he said and sat up fully. "Don't think it's love just because I'm the only man here."

Oh, that hurt. She got up, stormed over to her stuff, grabbed her jacket and shoved her arms in it. Then she wrapped her arms around her waist and tried to find some comfort in her own body heat. "It has nothing to do with you being the only man around. I've been around you for weeks now. I know you're a good man. You have a good heart." She glanced at him from across the fire. "When you fall in love with a woman, I just hope she's good enough for you."

"Beth—"

"I know, I fall in and out of love too fast." She sat down and tucked her own blanket around her. "I don't blame you for not believing me. Shoot, I wouldn't believe me if I were you."

Silence blew in like a cold wind around them and she huddle into her bed roll. "Good night, Quaid."

"Good night, Beth."

Beth stared at the dark shadows around them. Tomorrow she would arrive at Robert's doorstep. She felt years older than she was when she left Wisconsin. She had changed that much.

A cricket cried out in the nearby brush. A night owl called above her and she realized she wouldn't change back for all the world. Even if it meant she could take back her declaration of love to Quaid.

She'd get over it, she supposed, but the embarrassment would linger. She blew out a breath. Maybe everyone had it all wrong. Maybe she was the one who would become the old maid. How ironic would that be?

Tears filled her eyes and she brushed them away. The only time in her life when she wanted to hear the words *I love you* and they didn't come. She was aware of the great big space between her and Quaid. Aware that he kept it there.

He didn't believe her. He didn't believe she really loved him. He thought she had a fickle heart. Maybe she did. After all, she had run out on her own wedding just a few weeks earlier. This time was different though. Entirely different. This time she knew it would be all right if she lost her figure, if she had Quaid's children.

Quaid got up at the first streak of dawn and made a pot of thick black coffee. Beth lay with her head under her blankets. She had cried herself to sleep the night before. It had been a hard thing to listen to. All he wanted to do was go to her and comfort her and tell her he would take care of her the rest of her life.

But it wouldn't work.

He hadn't exactly lied to her. He'd simply let her make her own assumptions about things. Her assumptions were wrong. That told him a lot about the way she thought. She might have grit and determination now, but how will she be once they return to civilization?

In his experience he would be just a vague memory once she saw the number of men willing to cater to her every whim. She was a fickle gal. She'd see that soon enough once the local dandies came around with their sweet-talk and generous gifts. He remembered how she had told her father she couldn't disappoint them by choosing. Well, he wouldn't stand in her way.

He poured coffee into a tin cup and hunkered down by the fire. He had neither sweet talk nor generous gifts and still she claimed to love him. He almost believed her. That was the thing. He wanted to believe her. A man could get used to a woman mending his shirts and cooking his meals, filling his heart with her beauty and grace.

He could start to picture his house full of beautiful blue-eyed children with sable hair and pert noses. That was another sticking point. He couldn't imagine Beth wanting to get pregnant. Somehow he knew she would fret about her figure the whole time. Unlike her sister Maddie, who had a sweet Madonna-like smile on her face whenever she rested her hands on her enlarged stomach.

He glanced at the bundle of blankets that covered Beth. He wanted her. Wanted her to be his and only his. So he had to know. Had to know beyond a doubt that she wouldn't change her mind the first time another man smiled at her.

It was a mighty big struggle going on inside him. More than anything it made him angry. He tossed the dredges of his coffee on the flames and stood up. That was why he thought it was best to simply dump her on her brother's doorstep and walk away.

Let the other men come sniffing around. He would be patient and wait to see how her heart drifted. More than likely she would be breaking hearts all over three states by this time next month and he'd be headed to Kansas.

If he made it so that he couldn't see her then there would be no desire or temptation. No daily reminder of what he was missing. No frustration that he loved someone who could not give him what he wanted most—a home full of love and children who would hang on him and beg for his attention.

"Let's go, rise and shine. We can make your brother's ranch by noon if we scoot."

When she didn't budge he went over and toed the edge of her blanket. "Come on now, get up. You can lie abed at your brother's house."

Not a sound came from the blanket and Quaid got suspicious. He reached down and pulled it off her. Only Beth wasn't under the blanket. She had stuffed it with the packs from his mares.

With a muttered curse he stood and scanned the camp. Her saddle was gone and so was her mare. He hadn't checked for particulars when he got up. He simply glanced over to see if the horses were still around. They had been bunched up enough that he hadn't noticed one missing. Hadn't really thought to count noses.

He glanced toward the east. The sun had begun to rise, shooting pink and gold streaks into the deep dark blue of the early morning sky. It was blessedly cloud free. Venus hung low and sparkled along with a few other morning stars, giving one last twinkle before the sun blocked out their light.

He walked toward the horses and patted the stallion's nose. "How come you didn't let me know they left? Hmmm, old boy? Are we both getting soft?" He noted that she had walked her mare away from the camp. He tracked her path some one hundred yards out. She finally mounted and moved off toward the west and the rising mountains.

He blew out a long deep breath and knew he'd botched the whole thing badly the night before. It was the only reason she would have taken off alone. He allowed himself a moment to kick himself, then turned on his heel. He had a camp to dissemble and with any luck he'd catch up to her soon enough.

He'd see that she got safely to her home and then head toward his own place. He shrugged his shoulders and rolled his neck. It was painfully clear that tact was not one of his stronger points.

Beth grew more confident with every step. She had been riding for nearly two hours and Quaid was no where to be seen. She knew running off was the coward's way out, but then again he'd made it perfectly clear that he had no feelings for her. She wasn't used to having to argue or convince a man that she meant it when she said she loved him.

She shook her head. The heart was a fickle instrument indeed. She moved west toward the biggest peak.

Quaid had told her earlier that her brother's ranch was at the foot of the mountain. He said it was a half day's journey away. She had started out well before sunrise. The mountain now loomed large in front of her and she figured she was probably riding on her brother's land already.

What will Robert think when she comes sauntering up alone? She hadn't thought things through that far. Quaid would still have to come and bring the mares. Robert just might kill the guy for letting her ride on the prairie alone.

Beth frowned and fretted. She couldn't let that happen. She would simply tell Robert that she hadn't been able to sleep and had snuck off ahead. Yes, that should do the trick. How else would she go about explaining to her older brother that she had fallen in love with Quaid, but that he didn't return her love? Why, Robert may jump to conclusions and do something crazy like force Quaid to marry her.

Not that that idea didn't have some appeal. . . .

She couldn't do it. She would rather spend her life alone than force a man to love her when he clearly didn't.

After a time, she came upon a rider. He was dressed like a ranch hand and she figured he worked for her brother, so she waved him down.

"Helloooo." He stopped, tipped his hat and stared at her. She could barely make out his face under the shadow of the dusty brim. He wore a long-sleeved thick cotton shirt of deep navy, a pair of dusty pants, the legs of which were covered with leather chaps. His boots were firmly in the stirrups of his saddle. A six-shooter rested on his hip.

"Hello?" she called again.

He let her ride up close to him. His gaze never left her, but he didn't speak. It was almost as if he were a statue.

"Excuse me, is this the Bar M?" she asked. He blinked at her. She began to grow impatient. "I'm looking for my brother Robert Morgan. He owns the Bar M. I was told the house is at the base of the mountain." Silence. The ranch hand continued to stare at her as if he couldn't speak a word of English.

"Hello? Do you speak English? Se habla español?" She waved her hand in front of his face. "Whatever is the matter with you?"

"We don't see too many women out here," came a big rumbled voice from behind her. She turned in her saddle to find another hand, this one bigger and gruffer. He rode a lovely red gelding, one she recognized from her father's stock. "Fred's a bit tongue tied."

"I see." She frowned and for the first time was feeling truly uncomfortable about being alone. "I'm looking for my brother Robert. He's expecting me at any moment and I wanted to know if I was on the right track. It wouldn't do for him to have to come out after me."

"Nope, it sure wouldn't do," the man said and spit tobacco juice off to the side. He wiped his mouth. "The big house is just up ahead. Probably be a good idea for us to escort you there, since your "brother" is waiting for you."

"He is my brother," she said. She didn't like his tone at all or what he was implying. "And he'll be pretty upset with you if you do not treat me like a lady," she said with her chin raised.

"Is there some sort of problem?" Quaid asked. Surprised that he had come upon her so quickly, Beth turned to see Quaid glare at the two men. Relief took away from her embarrassment at seeing him again.

"I simply asked these men if I was on the Bar M and they were quite rude."

"It's nice to see you too," Quaid said and raised an eyebrow at her. Beth closed her mouth and took a deep breath. Somehow she had forgotten all her manners over the passed few weeks. "Harry, Fred, this is Miss Elizabeth Morgan. Beth, these are two of your brother's finest hands."

"Miss Morgan," they both said and removed their hats.

The bigger man nodded. "Didn't mean no disrespect, miss. We just don't git many females out in these parts. Especially females riding all alone."

"I'm not alone," she said quickly. "I came with Mr. Blair. Tell them, Quaid."

"I'll see she gets to the big house," Quaid said. "You boys get on with your chores."

"Yes, sir," the big man said and put his hat on. "Come on, Fred."

The younger man put his hat back on but his gaze never left Beth.

"Fred."

"Yes, sir." He finally moved his horse.

Beth felt better riding beside Quaid as they moved away. On one hand she was thrilled to see him, on the other she felt a bit miffed that he had managed to catch up with her so easily.

They rode in silence until they were out of earshot from the two men. "You always go riding up to strangers asking for directions?"

Beth didn't like the tone in Quaid's voice. He made her sound naïve and a bit silly. She knew it wasn't safe to ride up to strangers on the open prairie. "I'm not a complete bumblehead," she said and refused to look at him. "I assumed, correctly I might add, that I was already on the Bar M. The big man was riding one of our horses. So, I simply stopped to ask how much farther to the house."

"What if your assumption had been wrong?" His question was low and filled with an emotion she couldn't put her finger on. "What if these two were renegades? There isn't much protection in these parts for a woman riding alone."

"I have my pistol."

He sucked his teeth. The sound made her grind hers. She turned to him. "I'm fine. We're fine, and within moments I'll be at my brother's door and you will be happily rid of me." She waved her hand.

He reached out and grabbed her arm, stopping them both. She looked into his shaded eyes and her heart pounded. She saw something there besides anger, she saw concern and desire and maybe even need. Her mouth went dry and she tightened her hands on her reins.

"I'm not happy to be rid of you, Beth," he said, the words roughly. "Don't ever think I'm happy to be rid of you. My God, if anything ever happened to you, I don't know what I'd do. You're in me like a bad itch I can't scratch. If I had it my way, I'd haul you off that horse right now and keep you from ever getting to your brother's."

"Oh." It was the only thing she could think to say.

He let go of her with a shake of his head. "Darlin', you are the kind of woman who drives a man to drink. I can't believe I'm saying this, but—"

"Beth?! Beth is that you?" There was a loud whoop and Beth turned. She'd recognize Robert's profile anywhere. He sat atop a horse as if he were part of the creature and right now her brother barreled down on her like a mad man.

"Robert!" Her sheer delight at seeing a member of her family again brought tears to her eyes. He stopped his horse mere feet from her. It kicked up dirt as he dismounted. He reached up, grabbed her around the waist and hauled her down off her horse and into a bear hug.

Beth laughed as best she could when the stuffing was squeezed out of her. Then she hugged him back. He twirled her around, her feet never touching the ground. "What do you think you're doing coming all the way out here alone like this?" he scolded her when he finally stopped squeezing.

Beth pushed at his shoulders waiting for him to put her down. He didn't. Instead he held on to her and stuck his hand out. "Quaid, you old bear, thanks for seeing my sister safely here."

Quaid leaned down and shook it. "Morgan."

"She didn't give you much trouble did she?"

Beth gasped. He made it sound like she was a small child or a horse. "Hey!"

"She had her moments," Quaid said without batting an eye.

"Well, I've got her from here."

Quaid nodded, then without a second glance pulled his reins and moved off. Beth felt a tug of loss just before her brother laughed and tossed her in the air. She squealed like she did when she was a little girl and grabbed hold of Robert's shoulders.

"Put me down, you big lug."

"Not until you say the magic words."

"Oh, for goodness sake."

"Say them or I'll toss you again."

"No, don't . . . okay, okay. Robert Morgan, you are the best brother ever."

"Ever?" He started to lift her.

"Ever, ever," she said and smiled. "I promise, cross my heart, hope to die with sugar and a cherry on top."

"Good, there's my girl."

He put her down and wrapped his arm around her shoulders. "So, now that you're here, what's the first thing you want to do?"

"Take a bath."

"Well, it's not Saturday . . ." She grabbed hold of his arm and pinched. "Ow! Okay, we can make an exception."

She patted him and skipped a step. "I'm so happy to finally be here."

"Me too," he said. "You're clothes came about two weeks ago. I wondered what took you so long."

"Daddy and Quaid wouldn't let me take the train by myself and Quaid refused to move the horses by train. He said it was too dangerous for such beautiful animals."

Robert nodded. "Cars have been known to derail and tip. Not a pretty sight if you've ever seen it." He gave a small shudder and took her arm. "Here, I'll help you mount up. The house is just over that rise."

"I can mount by myself," she said with some pride. She'd been doing it for weeks now.

"Don't be silly," Robert dismissed her and, grabbing her by the waist tossed her up in the saddle. "Come on, I'll race you."

"Better hurry then," she said and took off. "I'm not waiting."

She kicked Buttercup into motion and flew across the pasture. She glanced behind her to see Robert swing one leg up and over and in a flash he was in the saddle and barely a yard behind her. She faced forward and urged her mare on. It was a happy moment and reminded her of being a young girl, full of carefree joy. They were neck and neck when she rounded the ridge and saw the house for the first time.

She knew in that moment that she was finally home.

Chapter Thirteen

"What can I do to help with dinner?" Beth asked. She had had the best afternoon of her life and she felt glorious. First she had taken a long hot bath and washed her hair. Then she had taken a nap in an actual bed with a feather mattress. Now she was dressed in her favorite dinner gown and felt flushed and prettier than she had felt in months.

She couldn't wait to see Quaid's reaction to how she looked all cleaned up.

"Whoooweee," Robert said low. "Beth, honey, you sure look different than the gal I found this morning." She blushed at his teasing and patted her hair.

"I clean up well, don't I?"

"That's a fact, plain and simple," Robert said. "It

looks like I'm going to have to hire a few extra hands just to keep the men off the property."

"Don't be silly," she said and smacked his arm. "Now, tell me what I can do to help with dinner."

"Don't you worry your head over dinner. I have a cook, remember? I introduced you to Garret this afternoon. He's about the best cook in the state, maybe west of the Mississippi."

"Why does he cook for you?"

"I pay him well and he's saving up to buy himself a place of his own."

"Well, then, I can set the table."

"Nope, no need. Mrs. Hansen the housekeeper does that. She's very handy to have around, and she has six kids, so this is a good job for her. Helps buy the family extras in town."

"I see. Then what can I do?"

"Well, you can go into town tomorrow and do some shopping. You like to shop, right? I'm told there's a nice dress shop run by a sweet widow."

"All right."

Beth stuffed the odd sense of disappointment down and moved toward the lace covered window. The parlor was small and cozy and obviously rarely used. "What do you do all day?" she asked as she looked out at the beautiful mountain range.

She heard the creak of a chair as Robert sat down. She pictured him balancing on two of the four legs as he was wont to do at home. Mrs. Poole was constantly after him to put all four legs on the floor.

"I'm running a ranch here, Kitten," he replied. "I've got livestock to look after, men to supervise, grasslands to cultivate and preserve, wells to dig, outbuildings to build, seasons to prepare for."

She turned and looked at her brother. "I don't want to be another burden to you, Robert. I've changed. I guess you could say I've grown up and now . . . now I want—no, I need to be a useful member of this family."

He dropped the chair onto all fours and stood up. "Aw, now honey, you have always been a useful member of the family. Why, just looking at you can make a man smile for a full day."

"There's more to me than my looks, Robert. Out on the trail I learned that I'm capable of doing useful things. I mean besides playing piano and shopping."

"But I love it when you play."

She shook her head. "Give me something to help with."

"I'm not going to make a washer woman out of you."

"Then let me run your household. I can take over the supervising of your cook and housekeeper. I can see to the groceries and the canning and the cleaning. It would be one less thing for you to worry about."

"You're my sister, Beth, not my wife. Look, you've been out on the trail for a long time." He got up and tapped the end of her nose. "You have a lovely tan to prove it. Why don't you take a few weeks to get some rest and see what things are like. Then we'll see if you still need work."

Beth blew out a long sigh. "But I—"

"Come on, dinner's ready." He took her arm. She knew the conversation was over. Her brother was a lot like her father in that manner. If they were done, then they were done and nothing more could be said to involve them in a subject.

She walked toward the dining room and was surprised to see only two plates set. "Is it just you and me for dinner?"

"Sure, I didn't think you'd be up to a party quite yet."

He held out her chair and she sat down. The table was lovely, set with a linen cloth, freshly pressed napkins and china she recognized as a set Robert had purchased the last time he was in Wisconsin. "Isn't Quaid dining with us?"

"Quaid? No, he—"

"Might be your foreman, but that doesn't make him a servant, Robert. He should be dining with you."

Robert sat down and studied her with a surprised expression. "Quaid isn't my foreman."

"Then your head wrangler, whatever—the least you could have done was invited him to dinner. After all, he brought you your horses all the way from Wisconsin."

"He didn't bring me any horses," Robert said and took his napkin out of the silver ring and put it in his lap. "Whatever gave you that idea?"

"Why, Pa gave him those mares to bring out to Wyoming. He hand selected those mares himself. I am certain they were meant for you."

"Are you talking about the horses that Quaid had tied to his stallion?"

"Yes."

"Those aren't my horses, Kitten."

"Then who did Quaid pick them up for?" she asked. Just then the housekeeper came into the room with a pot of soup and poured the first course in front of them. Beth's mouth watered at the scent of fresh chicken soup. She thanked the woman and dipped a spoon in her bowl. The flavor of rich broth and fresh chicken was pure heaven after weeks and weeks of trail food. "This is wonderful soup."

"Thank you. It was Garrett's mother's special recipe," the housekeeper said.

"I hope he'll share it with me," Beth said and took another spoonful. "I'd love to learn how to make it."

The housekeeper glanced at Robert who shrugged. "Sure," she said with a smile. "I'll let him know that you like it." Then she left the room.

"Maybe I'll take a bowl to Quaid," Beth said and took another sip. "Will he be staying in the long house tonight?"

Robert set down his spoon and studied her. "Beth, Quaid does not work for me. He's never worked for me."

"Why ever not? Papa trusts him and I can tell you he has a good hand with the horses." She frowned. "Your men treated him with respect. I thought he worked for you."

"Quaid Blair?"

"Yes, Quaid Blair."

"Kitten, Quaid Blair is one of the richest men west of the Mississippi."

"What?" She stopped her spoon halfway to her mouth. "I'm sorry I must be more tired from my trip than I thought. I could swear you just said that Quaid was one of the richest men west of the Mississippi."

"I did, because he is."

She dropped her spoon back into the soup and didn't even bother to blot the tablecloth. "I don't understand. Didn't Pa hire Quaid to bring your new stock out from Tennessee?"

"No, dumpling, Quaid and Pa were business partners when it came to the horses. In fact, I worked for Quaid the first year I came out here. He paid me enough to put down some good money on this spread."

"But he said he didn't have a home. I mean, he didn't want to put down roots in one place."

Robert laughed. "True enough he has about ten homes scattered around the west. His family owns two of the biggest shipping companies on the east coast. Quaid was the second oldest so he headed west after the war to see what was what. I heard he bought a couple of mines and made a fortune in silver and gold, then he turned to ranches and cattle. He helped finance one of the first cattle drives into Kansas City. Everything he touches turns to money. That's why I hooked him up with Pa on the last trip east for good stock. With Pa's horse sense and Quaid's luck I figure it's a good situation all ways around."

"Quaid's rich."

"Rich as Midas." Robert said and set down his spoon. Mrs. Hanson came in and removed their soup bowls and placed a lovely three bean salad in front of them.

"But he . . ." she sputtered. "He . . ."

"Doesn't like people to know he has money," Robert said and forked up his salad. "He told me once it changes the way people look at him."

She glanced at her plate and remembered how Quaid had commented that she had said yes to marrying Eric because of the size of diamond in her ring. "I guess that the ladies all want to catch his eye."

"Sure, all the socialites and wannabes. They figure the one who catches him will be set for life. Every time he goes into town he gets mobbed. I swear the women have some kind of lookout system in place. Before he dismounts there are at least three if not four ladies bustling around him and that is hard to do here. Trust me, the men outnumber the women here five to one."

"One would think a man would enjoy the attention."

"Not Quaid. Women see him only as a way to get rich quick. He's known it his whole life. I guess it's sort of made him who he is today."

"A lonely bachelor?"

"A man who knows what he wants and what he doesn't want," Robert said and finished his salad.

"What does he want?" Beth asked. She rested her elbows on the table, clasped her hands under her chin and leaned toward her brother. "I mean, for the sake of conversation. What do you think he wants?"

"I know what I would want if I were him."

"What?"

"A no-nonsense woman. Not some gal whose heart flutters in the wind. Someone steady. Someone who would love him for who he is, and stand by him even if he should lose every cent he owned."

"Has he ever told you what kind of woman he doesn't like?"

"Sure," Robert said and leaned back so that the housekeeper could take away the salad plate and place the main course in front of him.

Beth smiled at the woman as she took away the untouched salad and placed slices of warm ham and scalloped potatoes in front of her. "Well?" she asked when the housekeeper left.

Robert dug into the meat and potatoes. He chewed thoughtfully then swallowed. "It's kind of ironic, really. See, Quaid told me once that that last woman he'd ever fallen in love with was a socialite. If I remember right, he called them vain and self-consumed." Robert shrugged. "Guess he's a bit bitter."

Beth blew out a breath and picked up a fork. "Sounds as if he had his heart broken."

"Maybe," Robert said and took a long swig of his wine. "What man hasn't?"

Beth remembered the look on Eric's face when she had turned and fled the church. No wonder Quaid was in such a big hurry to get rid of her. She was everything he disliked in a woman.

She poked at the lovely meal. If she were serious about loving Quaid, she would have to change. Well, she had changed. Now all she had to do was prove it.

She was everything he'd ever wanted in a woman and he had let her go. Quaid lay in his bed and stared up at the darkened ceiling. "Idiot," he muttered. "Coward."

Truth was he knew that once word got out that Morgan's beautiful sister was in town every man in three states would be out to have a look. He didn't want to have to watch her revel in the attention. The last thing he wanted would be for her to bolt before she got halfway down the isle like she did the last time. Or worse to stay with him awhile, only to go off with the next handsome man who came along.

He blew out a breath. It really was all for the best. She might be made of sterner stuff than he once believed, but soon she'd be inundated with lovers. He wasn't the kind of guy who competed for a gal. Well, he wasn't.

He'd planned on wintering in Wyoming this year, but maybe he'd go spend some time with his folks instead.

His sister Sasha would help him forget the prettiest blue eyes west of the Mississippi. Wouldn't she?

Men started knocking on her brother's front door the very next day. Oh, they always had some bit of business or other, but Beth noticed how they looked about until Robert introduced them. She would smile and shake their hand and make conversation as she had been taught, but none of them were Quaid.

She watched for him everyday by the parlor window, but he never came. She smiled and nodded and played piano on command, always scanning the groups of arriving men for the one man she really wanted to see.

He stayed away.

Beth sighed. On the second week, she convinced Robert to take her into to town. As soon as she stopped near the mercantile there was already a group of men nearby, ready to help her off her horse. Help her cross the street. Help fetch and carry. They were all so sweet and yet they treated her as if she were helpless— precious yes, but helpless. Goodness. She couldn't understand why she used to like being treated this way. Now the men felt like flies hovering around her and she really truly wished they would just all go away.

She almost said so out loud. Then she realized it would be rude. So she smiled and nodded and stayed hidden in her brother's house. Is that how Quaid felt when he went into town?

She missed him. His laughter, his stubbornness, his

kiss. Beth sighed. Two days before she had sent an invitation to his place, asking him to come to supper. He hadn't come.

When she'd finally had enough, she got dressed in her new riding outfit and decided to take the bull by the horns. She rode to his place. When she crested a small ridge that separated the two ranches, she gasped. Quaid's land was lovely, but his home was even lovelier. It was built like a New England estate on the edge of a mountainous wilderness. Clapboard and shingles covered the outside. Lovely rose-colored shutters completed the look. There was a wrap-around porch and someone had planted roses in a bed nearby so that they climbed up the railing.

There were numerous outbuildings. A long house for the ranch hands. A smoke house. A stable and barn. Chickens scattered as she eased her horse up to the front of the house.

"I see you're making a habit of being stupid."

She turned to find Quaid leaning against the side of the house. He took off his gloves and eyed her from under the brim of his hat. "Hello to you too," she said and dismounted.

He walked over and took Buttercup's reins. "I thought your brother would have more sense than to let you wander off alone."

"Robert is not my keeper."

"Well, somebody needs to be." He gazed at her. His dark eyes were hot and full of light that warmed her stomach and made her tremble. She'd forgotten that. She'd forgotten how just looking at him could make her tremble.

"Are you volunteering for the job?"

He stepped closer and her stomach flipped. Lord, but she wanted him to answer yes. Instead he reached over and lifted her chin so that she looked directly in his eyes. "Miss me?"

"Yes," she said breathlessly. "I sent you a dinner invitation."

"I don't like crowds."

"It was only a few of the local ranchers. Robert invited them."

He stepped closer until only a breath separated them. "I don't have any use for the locals."

"Me neither." She caught herself squeezing her hands together and tried to relax, but he was so close. So close she could simply lean forward and kiss him. The tension was unbearable. It has been so long and her heart, no, her very soul missed him. "If you don't kiss me now, I think I'm going to die," she whispered. His eyes darkened and she threw all caution to the wind.

The kiss was instantaneous combustion. She wrapped her arms around his neck and dove into it. His hands were on her waist. His familiar scent filled her senses, warmed her. She knew she had come home and she was not going to let him tell her any differently.

Lord, but that man could kiss.

"What if I want ten children," he whispered against

her lips, then kissed her forehead, her cheeks, her nose before recapturing her mouth.

"Ten will be fine, but I can't promise I'll be up to making dinner every night if I'm chasing so many," she teased and kissed him back. She placed her hands on the sides of his face and peppered him with love.

"Okay, five children and dinner every night by six."

"All boys and dinner whenever it's done."

"All girls and dinner will get done by six."

"Four boys and a girl and a big lunch," she continued with her kisses as they negotiated. "That way there aren't a lot of dishes late at night."

"Two boys and three girls, who can help with the dishes."

"I want them all to go to college."

"My father will insist that the boys become sailors."

"My father will want them all to become horsemen."

He reached down and lifted her up into his arms. "We can settle this later. I mean to have years and years to figure this out." He strode toward the house, leaving Buttercup to wander away.

She wrapped her arms around his neck. "I always get what I want."

"Is that a fact?"

"Yes."

"And what is it that you want, Miss Elizabeth Morgan?"

"I want your heart."

He stopped at the edge of the porch and stared down

at her, his emotions clear on his face for her to see. "Are you absolutely certain about this?"

"I have never been so absolute." She pressed her hand to his cheek. "All I ever wanted was you."

He turned and kissed her palm. "Then marry me, my love, and you'll get both."

She rested her head against his shoulder. "Well, I suppose if I have to . . ."

He laughed, whirled her around and headed up the stairs only to be stopped by the sound of a shotgun being cocked.

They both turned to see Robert and five of his men on horseback staring down at them. Robert pushed his hat up and raised an eyebrow. "I don't think you'll be taking her anywhere without a preacher having some say over the matter."

"Robert!"

"It's okay, Sweetie," Quaid said and set her down. Her tucked her behind him none to gently, shielding her from the double barrels of lead pointed in their direction. "I mean to marry the gal, Morgan, and since she's said yes, there isn't much you can do to stop it."

Robert eyed them, scratched the side of his face a moment then signaled for the men to put away their guns. They did it reluctantly. "I kind of thought that might be the way of it," Robert said. "Beth's been moping around ever since you dropped her off."

Beth felt a hot blush rush up her neck and caress her

cheeks. Quaid glanced back at her and winked. Then he turned back to Robert. "I wanted to give her a chance to figure out what she really wanted. I'm not waiting any longer."

"Well," Robert said and sucked his teeth, "then it's a good thing I brought the preacher now, isn't it?"

"What?!" Beth looked around Quaid to see a man with a white pastor's collar being pushed to the front of the line of horsemen.

"What say we have a wedding?"

"I'm for it," Quaid said. He took Beth's hand and turned to face her. "Are you?"

She had a sudden flashback to the chapel in Boltonville and the way she had felt when she saw Eric at the end of the aisle. Was she about to make the same mistake? She did a quick search of her heart and realized that getting married had never felt so right. She smiled. "I'm ready."

The men whooped and hollered as they dismounted. Quaid squeezed her hand. "We can wait and have a proper church ceremony."

She reached up and caressed his cheek. "Nothing has ever felt this right. Let's do it now. I'm ready to come home."

She thought she saw tears gather in his eyes and he took off his hat. "Then let's get married."

The preacher stood on the front porch of that lovely house, surrounded by flowering rosebushes. The pink and white petals floated around in the breeze. Beth took

Quaid's hand and in front of her brother and his men said her vows. This time she said them with all the certainty that was in her heart.

This time she knew she had finally grown up and found a love that would last forever.

15653301R00119

Made in the USA
Charleston, SC
14 November 2012